YOURS, MI|

MW01127342

Addiction

H. E. LOGUE, M.D.

Outskirts Press, Inc.
Denver, Colorado

Contents

Foreword
by William Jerry Howell, M.D.

ADDICTION HAS BEEN said to be the most democratic and equally opportunistic disease in all of medical history. Addiction can affect an individual at any stage of life regardless of sex, race, education, or socioeconomic status. The beast of addiction can manifest itself in any form of normal human emotions, responses, and behavior. Addiction adversely affects and destroys the physical, mental, and spiritual well-being of every person it infects. Addiction is a potentially chronic relapsing disease, just like most chronic diseases recorded in medical history.

Recovery from addiction requires personal acceptance of this disease without any focus on the reasons why a person is addicted. Recovery is a process that takes time for the addict to develop successful coping skills, insight, and the strength necessary to battle the disease of addiction. The rewards of recovery are a new- found freedom from the bondage of addiction, and the addict's ability to accept life on life's terms without the need for alcohol, drugs, sex, gambling, or any other compulsive behavior.

In *Addiction: Yours, Mine, and Ours*, the author has so succinctly presented the characters, addictions, and message that the reader will empathize with the addicts' struggles yet yearn to understand addiction in these neighboresque people. You will want to know every insight developed through the book. You will consciously sense your evolving understanding of addiction and its awesome power. The unaffected public will have a welcome awakening to our collective responsibility to eradicate these destructive addictions. A special vigilance will emerge for family and friends.

Although much has been written previously on addiction, Dr.

Logue's novel, *Addiction: Yours, Mine, and Ours*, is a new important paradigm of understanding addiction through the medium of entertainment. His novel gives us realistic characters in a true-to-life storyline which intensely appeals to both our individual and collective motivation to become part of the solutions.

I am particularly pleased to have offered personal reflections and content suggestions for Chapters 30 and 31. Anytime we can fight ongoing addiction problems, we should not hesitate.

Acknowledgments

My fortune as an author is to have the counsel and assistance of numerous professionals and friends who believe in the value of this book becoming available to the public. I extend heartfelt appreciation to the following:

To my wife, Kathy Logue, R.N., who tediously edited for format, content, literary correctness, and readability.

To Tamara V. Shadinger, Ph.D. for patiently enduring many iterations; for research, artistic assistance, and logistical considerations.

To William Jerry Howell, M.D. for his interview, which imparted invaluable information, and his reading of the manuscript and giving his expert feedback.

To Steve Briggs, founder of the Freedom Source.

To Marc D. Feldman, M.D. for reading the manuscript and providing excellent feedback.

To Beverly Penny, R.N., psychiatric nurse, for her interview and providing insight from the nursing perspective.

To the many others who read the manuscript and provided professional or lay readership and valuable feedback, including: Lita A. Clark, Ph.D., C.E.A.P., S.A.P.; Charles L. Joiner, Ph.D.; Judith Vercher, L.M.F.T., L.P.C.; Gerald K. Anderson, Ph.D.; Richard Ince, Ph.D.; Kay McLean, M.S.N., R.N., P.M.H.C.N.S.-B.C.; (and her reading club); Alan S. Blackwell; Maureen Gleason, and Kim Potter, founder of the Chris Sidle Foundation.

To Peggy Holly and Dianne Moore, M.H.T., for their ever available general help.

To my patients and colleagues for their interest, encouragement, and support.

Introduction

THIS IS A novel about life, and people much like you and me. You will find parts of me in it. You are likely to find bits and pieces of yourself. The characters will reveal for you, show, and teach you things you never knew about addiction. You will learn how to recognize addiction, understand it, and treat it. Yet all you will be doing is reading a realistic novel of people and their lives, people like those I see in my office every day.

The book is about addiction(s) and their influence on our behavior and damage to our health and to those we love. We will cover most recognized addictions. Smoking, alcohol, and opiates (the big three) are the most visible of the problematic addictions, and therefore are used as a basic model for illustration and educational purposes. This is a fictional story written for the purposes of entertainment and self-help as well as personal and public education. You will be better equipped to win your battle over addiction or to help a friend or loved one.

Addictive substances are generally seductive, much as sex itself can be addictive. Intense, immediate pleasure is often the hook that tethers us to that addictive source of pleasure. It will seem so innocent, and feel so delightfully powerful, that our minds are captured. This combination is irresistible to many, unleashing a passion within us, igniting an unquenchable fire of desire. With some addictions this is even instantaneous, but with others, time and denial collude to eventually addict us. We are lulled into believing that we have control of the fire. We forget that fires can also deceptively and slowly destroy us.

With bravado, we swing our sticks of fire much as cavemen might have swung their fire weapons attempting to impress their women or peers.

Tobacco releases tars, nicotine, and other chemicals into the body. Nicotine is a powerful nervous system stimulant. Tars are carcinogenic irritants to the oropharynx, larynx, trachea, and lungs. Statistics attribute 440,000 deaths annually in the US alone directly to smoking and exposure to secondhand smoke.[1] The statistics regarding other addictions are equally disturbing (please see Appendix I).

Treatment is available for all addictive disorders. The storyline engages these, thereby teaching us about them. After reading the book, see Appendix II for further sources of information.

Ignorance plus addiction equals destruction, generally through early and discomforting illnesses that range from tooth decay and loss, impotence, and personality changes to more serious ones that frequently cause premature death. Knowledge helps one to understand and remove the addictive control, thereby avoiding ill-health, and postponing death until its natural fate and time.

This book is for those of you who are personally addicted, know someone who is, or would appreciate being more informed. You will begin to know and identify addicted people, their struggles, addiction, its consequences and, most important, recovery and the maintenance thereof. It sparks the motivation, hope, and desire for recovery and gives the formula to win the battle.

Read on, if you suspect that you or anyone you know has any addiction.

---

1   Although the time frame referenced is 2000-2002, the knowledge and facts are up to date as of 2009.

ADDICTION
Yours, Mine, and Ours
We Can and Must Overcome

Here's How
New and Necessary Insights

CHAPTER 1

Face Reality

BRIAN WAS FIVE years old, but his quizzical nature was about to blindside his Papa Sam Robbins by forcing him to an uncomfortable acceptance of his own tenuous mortality.

Since recovering from his recent surgery to remove lung cancer, this was Sam's first outing with his adorable and only grandson. Having just finished Brian's favorite game, miniature golf, they were continuing their routine post-game visit at an ice cream parlor in Crestline Village.

"Papa," Brian began, matter-of-factly, as children are prone to do when they obliviously plunge innocently into serious matters of the human psyche, "are you going to die?"

It was the question itself, not the ice cream, that sent a chill through Sam's spine and heart. To him, it seemed that Brian was unusually concerned for his age, which made it obvious to Sam that his own emotion must be subdued and Brian's doubt and insecurity allayed. He would need strong, authoritative reassurance. Sam needed to deliver.

"Of course not. We've got lots of games to play and ice cream to eat and years to go before you're grown. Don't worry; the doctors are taking good care of me. You almost beat me today, so we'll play again next week. Okay?"

"I'm going to win next time."

"I bet you will."

They had nearly reached Brian's home when Sam realized that he had become silent and withdrawn. Doubt and negative projections were enveloping him. He especially couldn't accept having to die before Brian was grown and all because he had been stupid enough to keep smoking, even after learning that smoking causes cancer. These thoughts and feelings fed his growing guilt and self-incrimination. Soon he was having difficulty sleeping; he was waking up early, and worrying endlessly. His energy seemed to be unreachable. Sam was depressed.

Sam's wife, Kitty -- his nickname for Caroline -- had always been the ear he could turn to. At times, she would intuit his need and offer to "talk about it." Sometimes Sam would swallow his pride and ask Kitty, "Honey, can we talk?" Today he confided to Kitty, "I've been low as a snake's belly ever since Brian asked me if I was going to die."

"Brian did that?"

"It really shook me. I just feel beat and tired. Is there any use in trying?"

"Samuel Robbins, you just quit that talk right now. I know you feel bad, but you're just getting over lung surgery. The doctors tell us that they got it all; now, believe them. You need to see Dr. Lavoy." She was referring to a psychiatrist known to both of them. "If cancer didn't get you, we're sure not going to let depression get you." She insisted, and made the appointment.

As Sam sat in Dr. Lavoy's waiting room, he felt conspicuous. *I thought I would be the last person to wind up in a shrink's office*, he thought. His face could have been a poster for sadness, the antithesis of his usual gregarious personality. Depression was robbing him of life even more than the cancer.

Sam had been a walking definition of life, being always upbeat and positive. He seemingly looked for opportunities to help others and, for that matter, even his country. At eighteen, he had joined the Marines and served four years, eighteen months of which were in Vietnam. He rarely mentioned his service and never discussed it.

At one point he mentioned to Kitty that he never smoked or drank alcohol while at home. He would not have disappointed his Dad or "Mama Beth," the family nickname for his mother. In the service it was much different from high school, where he was six foot one, good-looking, and popular. There had always been plenty to do.

In the Marines, it was train, train, and more training -- and just being a Marine. Most socializing was done while smoking cigarettes and drinking beer. Alcohol had never been that important to him, but cigarettes had hooked him hard.

After returning from Vietnam, Sam used the GI Bill to go through college at the University of Alabama in Tuscaloosa. There he met Travis MacInough. They became best buddies throughout college and life. Both of them married and lived in Birmingham, Alabama. Travis pursued construction, mostly building houses, while Sam developed a companion business of asphalt paving. Their friendship and joint efforts remained intact through the years.

Life had been mostly good until now. Purpose and meaning had become empty words. It seemed that everything was slipping away from him.

"Mr. Robbins," Dr. Lavoy called to Sam, "would you come with me, please?"

Sam looked across the desk at Dr. Lavoy. He had succumbed to Kitty's pleadings. He was aware that he needed to talk. Not just for cathartic value, but to inform Dr. Lavoy of pertinent information. Otherwise, the advice he was seeking might well miss the mark. One must know the target before taking aim. *But it's not easy to just open my mouth and start telling this man my unflattering personal blemishes. I wonder what he already knows about me, anyway. I have to start somewhere. I can't waste the session.*

As if reading his mind, Dr. Lavoy spoke. "What is most on your mind today, Mr. Robbins?"

"I've got so much to talk about, ask about. I should have come when I first realized cigarettes were bad for my health and that I was addicted, but I didn't. Now I have lung cancer. I waited too long.

My nodes were negative. They might have gotten it all. I feel guilty. I brought this on myself.

"I should have come when my niece, Eileen, whom you treated, was diagnosed with Bipolar Disorder and we learned that she inherited it through my brother, Herschel, her father, but I didn't. And now I'm depressed. I don't know if it's because I've got cancer or whether I have Bipolar Disorder or both.

"I should have come when I realized my nephew, Thomas, was drinking too much, partying too much, too irritable, too moody. I used denial, just as he did. I waited too long. He drank everything he could buy and slept with every girl who would say yes. Then one of the girls got pregnant and she refused to have an abortion. It ruined his chances with Sue, a wonderful high school sweetheart. He almost killed himself with drinking and overdosing before he finally got help.

"So, I'm finally here. Can you help me, Doc? What do I need to do? My five-year-old grandson thinks I'm going to die. What made me smoke those things all those years?"

Lavoy replied, "There are many reasons why people smoke, even knowing the risk. As we know you better, we'll likely be able to figure out why you smoked. Are you comfortably tobacco-free at this time?"

"After getting cancer, I can safely say I'm through with smoking."

"Fine, but we'll talk about it further to make sure. We also need to address your depression. It's going to get in the way of anything else you might need to do. Is the depression interfering with your daily activities? How is your sleep?"

"I'm not nearly as sharp or productive as I used to be. I often do have trouble going to sleep; and, of course, I get up to empty my bladder. Then I wake up early and can't go back to sleep."

"Are you having any thoughts that it just doesn't matter anymore? That you wouldn't care whether you wake up or not?"

"Sometimes, but I'm not thinking of...you know...doing away with myself."

"Have you had any thoughts of harming yourself?"

"Sure. We all think about it."

"Have you thought of ways to do it? Or made any plans to take your life?"

"No, no, no, nothing like that. I mean, I know how I'd do it, but I don't plan to."

"Sam, we need to have a contract right now that at any time, if you're thinking seriously or strongly about harming yourself, you'll call me first, and if I'm not immediately available, you'll go to the emergency room and have them call me and tell them what's on your mind."

"That's no problem. You have my word."

"Are you at a point where you have lost interest in your usual activities or maybe even the purpose for living?"

"Somewhat -- what makes you ask that?"

"Call it a hunch, but it's not uncommon among people who are depressed. But in you, it's leading me to a different thought process. You see, you were mentioning having so much guilt from smoking all those years, but you also talked about concern for your children and your wife. I believe that if you reestablish a purpose and put some energy in that direction, it will be therapeutic in helping you fight the depression. It will also help you stay focused and help you not to relapse into smoking again."

"Is that right?"

"It is; everything really works together. I'm going to give you a prescription for Celexa. Take one each night at bedtime. You need to be active. Activity helps the circulation of the blood and the chemicals. Take walks, play with your grandson, eat out, just do things."

"I'll have to push myself," Sam replied, almost protesting.

"Then push hard," Lavoy ordered. "That's a prescription and I expect you to do it. I'll see you in a couple of weeks."

With the meeting ended, Sam proceeded directly to the pharmacy and filled his prescription. He wanted to get started that night. It was midafternoon when he left the pharmacy. He drove directly to Brian's house. This was the wonderful part of being retired. He took pleasure in being unrestrained and being guided by his impulses.

Brian was home from kindergarten, so Sam could accomplish his mission of seeing him and would also talk to him about the evils of smoking. As a bonus, he would get to see Peggy, his daughter.

Peggy, now forty-three, looked the picture of health, seemed always happy, and today, as from her infancy, adored Sam and made him swell with pride as if nothing made her happier than to be in his presence. She was pleased, and not amazed, that he had "popped in" unannounced and was glad to offer him a glass of "sweet iced tea."

"Hey Brian, sit on Papa's knee. Ride the horsey. What do you know about smoking?"

"Smoking is bad and made my Papa very sick. Mama and Daddy don't like smoking. I hate smoking."

"All right, that's great. Papa didn't know better, but Brian knows better, right?"

"I know better. Papa, you promised to take me fishing. Can we go, please?"

Sam relaxed, being reassured of Brian's solid indoctrination against smoking. Wanting to reward Brian, Sam impulsively answered, "Yes, we will go fishing, Brian. The doctor says I need to do things, so let's go fishing. I'll check at home, but I think we can go Saturday."

Peggy brought in the tea. Brian was off and headed to his next interest as if cued by telepathy.

"How's Mama doing?" Peggy asked.

"Oh, just fine. But Kitty's mother is getting up in years and hardly gets out and about anymore. Her rheumatism is getting bad. I'm afraid it's beginning to wear on your mother's nerves. It might be a good idea to see her a little more often, if you could. For support, you know."

"No problem, Dad, glad to do it. Thanks for the heads up. By the way, speaking of grandparents, cousin Eileen called. She might be a little high. She's got this new project. This one sounds pretty good, though. Her ideas are always so infectious. Your own Mama Beth is now 92, so before it's too late, she says we need to have a family reunion. Of course, she's got it all figured out. We'll all meet in Decatur, Alabama on Friday afternoon and evening. She figures we'll all meet for breakfast on Saturday and then head out to the Marshall Space Flight Museum in Huntsville. It'll be awesome, she says. She will charter a bus for the family and we'll take a guided tour of the tri-cities area on Sunday before we all head home."

"Well," Sam offered, "that's Eileen for you. She has it all figured out. But hey, it sounds good to me. Just get me the details. Oh, Brian says he would like to play more miniature golf with me. Would that be okay with you?"

"That's fine."

"You heard Brian ask to go fishing. I'd like to take him Saturday if it's okay with you. Would you like to join us?"

"Sounds like men stuff to me."

"Okay. Don't say we didn't offer."

At home Sam related to Kitty the substance of the meeting he had with Dr. Lavoy. He talked of doing what he was instructed to do. He told Kitty Dr. Lavoy wanted him to be active and that Brian could probably help with that. When he mentioned taking Brian out on the boat, Kitty was concerned.

"Don't you think it might be a little soon to go on a boat? What if you get stranded or something? You don't have all your strength yet."

"Doc told me to push myself hard. He said I needed it."

"Okay, just be careful," she directed him.

CHAPTER **2**

Overboard

SAM'S INTERNAL CLOCK woke him ten minutes before sunrise on Saturday. His anticipation of taking Brian fishing on Smith Lake had been building for at least an hour. Sam expected to be at his favorite fishing hole by 7:15. Today was unusual in that Sam had managed to have solo custody of Brian for Friday night and Saturday.

Brian was just about the cutest boy he had ever seen and looked just like his mama, Peggy, which meant, of course, that the Robbins in him was dominant. That pleased Sam. Brian was of average height for his age, at three foot one, and had a slim build, weighing forty pounds. His hair was sandy blond and his eyes hazel. Everyone, even non-family and strangers, thought he was the most adorable little boy. Brian was both energetic and inquisitive, a combination that was sure to keep Sam on his toes.

Sam's retreat was a spacious and comfortable lake house on a point with its own private pier. Sam made breakfast and prepared lunch before waking Brian. Sam's excitement and enthusiasm about getting up to Smith Lake was not missed by Brian. He too was eager to get to the boat and began immediately peppering Sam with questions about the boat and fishing. Sam hurried and only rinsed the dishes before loading the boat.

As they gently moved out into the lake with the motor idling, both Sam and Brian were quiet. It was a surreal moment, as if both were

9

tuned into some instinctual connection with water and nature. Brian was feeling total joy and adventure, as if a new world had opened up to him. Sam felt more as if he were floating away from the cares and stress associated with solid ground. Brian exclaimed that the lake was "as big as an ocean!"

"Not quite that big," Sam answered. "But some say that Smith Lake is the prettiest and cleanest lake in Alabama."

To Sam's delight, Brian pretended to assist in piloting the boat from time to time on their short journey to the "fishing hole." Once there, they dropped anchor and Sam began telling Brian all he needed to know about fishing. Very important was the need to be quiet. Sam would show him how deep to set the hook, how to watch the cork, and when to jerk the line. He would show him which type of bait to use. Sam even promised Brian to teach him how to clean the fish and prepare it for cooking.

Only one other boat had gone past them after they anchored. Sam recognized Mr. Biddle, who acknowledged their presence and friendship with his customary wave and a nod of the head. Sam showed Brian how to respond. One other boat came into view headed their way.

Sam saw that Brian had his line in the water and was watching the cork before going forward to the portside of the boat. Brian remained at the rear on the starboard side, intently watching his line with the float gently bobbing up and down. Suddenly it disappeared under the water.

"Papa, I've got a big one."

When his rod jerked, Brian lost his footing and tumbled overboard, holding onto the rod. Sam had turned just in time to see Brian's feet disappearing over the side. He took two quick steps and went headfirst, clothes, boots, watch, wallet, everything. Thrashing frantically around, he felt his left hand touch something. Maybe it was a shoulder. But then he couldn't find it. It was gone. But in which direction? Down, yes down. He swerved to his left and with all his strength headed deeper. He saw movement and gave a powerful stroke with his hands and bumped into Brian. He hugged Brian with his left arm and stroked down hard with his right arm. When he tried to kick with his feet, they wouldn't move. Something was holding them. They were tangled in the fishing line. He fought furiously to get to the surface. Fear that he could not save Brian squeezed more adrenaline into his bloodstream. He had not yet even thought of himself.

Sam struggled and fought furiously toward the light. Finally their heads broke through the surface and they began to gasp for air. Sam was desperately fighting hard with his one arm to tread water when he heard a motor and turned to see that the passing boat had changed course and was speeding toward them.

"Sam, Sam, are you all right?"

"I'm in trouble! We need help!" Sam saw that it was Jim and Julia Goodson, headed down from their cabin which was a quarter mile upstream.

"What's wrong? Here, hand me the boy. Are you all right?"

"My leg's tangled in the fishing line."

"No wonder you were fighting that water so hard. Give us your hand. We'll get you on board." They were able to reach Sam's belt and, pulling together, heaved him into their boat.

Julia's full attention now was focused on Brian, who was frighteningly quiet and shivering. She dried him and wrapped him in her bright red beach towel. With her soft voice, she reassured him and held him close to share her body heat. His worries melted on her like butter on a hot roll. Sleep would have been a welcome escape, but he was now wishing his mama was there.

Jim was helping Sam get settled into the boat and Sam was beginning to regain his composure and talk as if it had been just another day. Glancing at Brian and Julia, he was reassured by Julia's motherly skills with Brian. *Better than I could do,* he thought.

"Thank God you guys came over. With the fishing line, I just couldn't have held on very long and we would both have been goners. That was too close for comfort."

"I was aiming for my fishing hole, but Julia looked over and recognized your boat. She was waving at you when she saw you go overboard. We just figured whatever the reason, it couldn't have been a good one, so we just gunned it and headed over here. You look as if you could use a cigarette. Here, I've got some Marlboros. Have one."

"Thanks Jim, I think I'll take you up on that offer. I've been quit for five years, but I could sure use one now."

Brian began to cry and pleaded, "Papa, don't smoke! I don't want you to die."

Stunned, Sam declined. "You're right, Brian. No cigarette is worth my life."

Jim returned the pack to his pocket without taking one for himself.

"I'm mighty obliged y'all came over." Sam felt the line tug on his leg. Realizing that it could be the fish, he began to pull the line in hand over hand. "I believe we might still have a fish on the line." While it seemed like a half a day, eventually Sam pulled in a pound and a half bass and got in on board. "Hey Brian, look at the size of this bass you caught! What about rewarding our rescuers with it? I believe our fishing's probably over for today." Sam then began reeling in the rod and reel still attached to the other end of the line.

Sam, for the two of them, effusively praised the Goodsons for their efforts and for saving their lives. He promised to be there for them and find a way to repay them, but hoped for all concerned it would not be "in kind."

Back in their boat and headed to the lake house, Sam and Brian talked about the event. Sam wanted to construct the thinking and the memory, so that Brian's Show and Tell to his class, and especially to his mother, would not prevent further opportunities for them to go out together. That would be more devastating than his cancer had been. He was already thinking about finding the courage to do another fishing trip so that Brian could have a better experience. He vowed to never go on a boat again without everyone wearing a life jacket.

CHAPTER 3

Positive Idea

SAM RETURNED TO Dr. Lavoy for his two-week first follow-up visit. He had a conscious internal debate as to whether or not to mention the boating incident to Dr. Lavoy. He decided to just let the conversation flow and he would mention it only if it seemed appropriate.

Samuel Robbins was an affable and confident man, who was strikingly different in personality from his more taciturn brother, Herschel. His niece, Eileen, Herschel's daughter, had always liked him and her personality was, in fact, more like her uncle Sam's than her father's. Except for church and weddings, he dressed casually, but always neat with crisp, clean attire and traditional grooming. Even now, at sixty-eight years old, he was in good physical shape, showing no hint of his recent encounter with "the big C."

Sam was a smart -- as opposed to shrewd -- businessman. Clients were comfortable with him. He was down to earth, humble, and honest in his dealings with everyone. His reputation was solid. He exuded believability.

Being retired was not his idea of "a quality life." His custom was one of being constantly productive and of helping his family, his friends, his business, and associates. He did everything with a strong spiritual underpinning. Being forced to slow down because of his illness, his surgery, and his treatments had cramped his usual energetic style and even his psyche. Now he was feeling some hope that indeed

Dr. Lavoy might help him refocus his life and renew his energy. Sam dared to think, *Perhaps I could become an anti-smoking crusader.*

Now that Sam's depression was lifting, he was reclaiming his belief that a positive attitude and a life of helping and giving to others are powerfully therapeutic in maintaining good health -- fighting cancer, most illnesses, and, he would say, even addiction.

Dr. Lavoy welcomed Robbins to his consultation office twenty minutes late, but as the last patient of the day, they could be unhurried in their discussions. He had been looking forward to today's visit with excitement, sensing that Robbins shared a passion of his: a war on addictions. He felt Robbins would be a wonderful spokesperson who could deliver a poignant message. He was able to engage emotion, where the strength of the fight to overcome strong cravings resides. It would be fighting fire with fire: confidence against stubborn resistance. *Robbins could do that and I could be satisfied with helping him.* His intuition would be validated to learn that Robbins was having similar thoughts.

"How are you? Are you feeling better about yourself, your future? Are you sleeping better? How's your mood?"

"I must be better. I've been busier, as you suggested. My mood is definitely improved. I sleep better. My energy and interests have improved. My wife says I'm better. That medication is great stuff. I did listen to you. I have been busy."

"I am glad you heard me. Your activity has augmented the effect of the medicine; I'm sure it's helping you. However, connecting with an interest, deciding to pursue it, and then engaging in the follow-through is the unwritten prescription that unlocks your natural chemicals, neurotransmitters, and wakes you up to the joy of life and opportunities. Welcome back."

Lavoy continued, "You need to continue taking your medicine. Studies show a high relapse rate in people who discontinue their medicine early. We will be monitoring your symptoms closely. If you do well, since this is your first depressive episode, we might taper you off the medicines, but with caution and not anytime soon."

Sam acknowledged the good news. "I don't like taking medicine, but I do like feeling good."

Dr. Lavoy satisfied himself that the chosen treatment was appropriate and working. He complimented Sam on following his instructions to be busy.

"It actually got a little too busy and scary when I took Brian fishing." Sam gave a succinct account of the boating incident.

Lavoy offered advice. "Sam, you need to be more careful. When people are depressed, they often make bad decisions. It sounds as if you prematurely took on this adventure, maybe out of guilt; you even forgot the life jackets. You were probably trying too hard to reassure and please Brian. I applaud your initiative, but do be careful."

Sam was listening. "Your point is on target and well-taken, Doc."

Lavoy answered, "Good. Why don't you tell me how and when you quit smoking? Then I'll tell you about the idea I have."

"That's fair enough. When I finally quit for good, it was 1995. I drove up to Muscle Shoals, Alabama to see my mother, Mama Beth, as we call her. It is short for Bethany. Her full name is Sarah Bethany Burns Robbins. She always accuses her parents of trying to double dose her on religion, with two of her names taken from the Bible. Frankly, we all thought it worked pretty well because as far as any of us know, she never drank or smoked, and no one will admit ever hearing her utter a cuss word."

Lavoy listened intently. The more he learned about this family, the more he could understand the various individuals in the family. He had, of course, treated Sam's niece, Eileen, for more than three decades. He always perked up to hear more about her family tree.

"Mama Beth was eighty-seven at the time, still sharp as a tack and able to get about just fine. I should have known I couldn't fool her, but I tried. When I was nearing Tuscumbia, I decided to have one last cigarette before reaching the family home. I would just leave the pack in the car so she wouldn't be able to see it.

"My baby sister, Daisy Jane Robbins Hull, lives with Mama Beth. Now hers is a tragic story. She didn't move to Birmingham like us boys, but stayed in the Muscle Shoals area and married respectably. She and her husband both worked. They had a beautiful baby girl four years into their marriage. When she was two years old, she caught the measles and they went to her brain and she died. Sis was never the same after that and her poor husband, Bobby, just drank himself to death over the next couple of years. So, Sis just moved back in with Mama Beth and they've lived there all this time, looking out for each other. Anyway, I know I'm rambling, but recalling all this is meaningful for me."

"Cathartic, maybe?" replied Lavoy.

"Perhaps. I just know at 92, Mama Beth is not likely to be with us much longer. I guess I feel some guilt for not going up more often than I do. The community thinks she's a bit eccentric, but everybody loves her. She's a great storyteller. The young people are attracted to her and spellbound at the stories she can spin. I'll get one of her stories for you.

"At any rate, I left my cigarettes in the car and went in to visit. I gave them both a hug and we chatted for a few minutes. I accepted an offer of some hot tea even though Mama Beth knows full well that I prefer coffee. Just as I started to drink my tea, she said, 'Samuel, I thought you were going to quit that habit of smoking!' Now, at the time I didn't realize how she had picked up on it so easily. But now that I've been quit for a few years, I fully understand how non-smokers pick up on the presence of smokers. Frankly, I'm embarrassed that I was so ignorant and stupid about myself all those years that I smoked. So I told Mama Beth that I had honestly tried. In fact, I had quit several times, at least three or four, sometimes as long as a whole year. Invariably, I would think that I had earned the right to have just one, so I would, and then I could not resist resuming my habit.

"Undaunted, Mama Beth responded with a question. 'Samuel, where were the signs when you quit?'

"I asked her, 'What signs?'

"'I told you before, you need to read the almanac, boy. How do you get anything done without following the guides in the almanac?

I just don't know about you young folk.'

"'I just never believed in that stuff and I don't understand it. Where are the signs supposed to be when we quit, Mama Beth?'

"'If you want to quit smoking for good, you need to quit when the signs are below the knees.'

"'Is that a fact?' I stalled.

"'It's a fact, son.'

"'Thank you, Mama Beth.' I awkwardly ended the conversation. I didn't offer a promise to follow up. I'm sure that my tone sounded rather like a mixture of arrogance and condescension. I immediately felt guilty.

"Mama Beth had riled my emotions and gotten me a little mad. I knew it was because I was disappointed in myself and my inability to kick the habit. I left earlier than I had intended and drove over to Wheeler Dam and Locks. I wanted to be someplace undistracted by driving. This place had always fascinated me. Doc, did you know that Wheeler Dam and Locks are historic? The Tennessee River dropped 100 feet right there where the locks are built. It made the river impossible to navigate. They built a lock and dam to cover the entire hundred feet. Big barges and ships go into one end of it and rise or fall 100 feet in one operation. It is similar to the Panama Canal Locks, but this one is the height of a ten-story building and to this day it remains the highest single one-step operation in the entire world. I just stood there and watched the water rise and lift up those huge barges and I thought, *If we can overcome obstacles like this, surely I can put my mind to it and quit smoking.*

"But you know what? I got an almanac and I waited until the signs were below my knees before I stopped again. I've never smoked another one. That was in '95."

"That's a very interesting theory and one I've previously never heard. One day I'll put that one in a book," said Lavoy.

The two men were bonding. They were two ex-smokers talking about a common problem and a common interest. Lavoy was emboldened to broach the subject of collaborating with Sam to fight addiction.

"Now for the idea that I wanted to mention to you. Why don't you turn your guilt into a positive force rather than a negative force? Someday, I'll tell you how I quit smoking. There are many people out there with many different ways to quit smoking. You could gather some of those stories, then put them in a book. Tell the world the problems with addictions, the consequences of addiction, the mechanism of addiction, the power of addiction -- but also the varied and successful ways that people can overcome addictions. Notice I use the plural. There are many types of addictions besides tobacco. There's alcohol, narcotics, opiates, sex, gambling, the internet, running, racing, and many others. Their similarities and differences will be explained later. Basically, anything that produces intense pleasure can be addictive.

"I should think it would be rather fun to gather some of those stories, and richly rewarding to be able to utilize them to make an impact on others who need to know why they're addicted and how to quit their dependence. The first key is detoxing from dependence on the substance of addiction. But dependence and addiction are partners and remain with you for life, just like an allergy, which can and will come back with a vengeance. Detox techniques are individually designed according to the substance and even the person's situation. Obviously there are fundamental physiological and psychological differences between addictions to running and narcotics, etc. However, the similarities are sufficient to include them all under the broad heading in our discussions."

"Doc, that's worth thinking about. I've wondered if there was some way I could help people stop smoking, but I didn't have a clue as to how to go about it. I'm going to give some serious thought to this."

"Think about it as a new prescription, okay? It's an interest of mine, so I would be quite happy to help you. I'll see you again in a couple of weeks and I'll be curious to know if you've learned about any other unusual techniques to quit smoking." It was a rhetorical comment, but Sam would surprise him.

CHAPTER **4**

Excitement

LAVOY WAS IN a creative mood. Samuel Robbins' enthusiasm had inspired him to rekindle his dormant ambition to write about addiction. The public must have an affordable, workable method to learn about addiction and, just as importantly, a user-friendly manner to overcome it. He sensed that Sam could and would become a key figure in this reawakened mission. Sam and Dr. Lavoy were now inspiring each other to pursue a mutual interest.

Robbins had been his last patient that Wednesday morning. A solid, gray sky enveloped his office and all of Birmingham. Not ready to relinquish his hopes of an afternoon golf game, he walked to the window, looking for sunshine at the edge of the cloud, but it reached to the horizon. At that moment, a lightning bolt flashed across the sky and was followed quickly by a thunderclap. He mused, *I'll take that as a sign. That is a flash of energy and a thunderous applause to start my project this afternoon. No better time than now to start my manuscript. It's a sublimation reward for taking a golfing rain check.*

Foraging through the office kitchen, he found enough leftovers and snack material for a small lunch. Wasting no time, he was savoring the last morsel and bringing his Dr. Pepper with him as he opened the "catchall closet."

Sure enough, in the midst of boxes of old, outdated educational tapes, umbrellas with broken ribs, pharmaceutical giveaway trinkets, unhung awards, and other dubious items, there was the cardboard Hale orange crate labeled simply, "Smoking." He gave an audible sigh of satisfaction. Some of the items in this treasure trove had been languishing patiently for more than two decades, waiting for this moment.

Lavoy began sorting the items into stacks of newspaper articles, medical journal articles, personally written thoughts and ideas, and anecdotal vignettes into separate piles. Everything in the box related to addiction, most of it to smoking.

Education was the key, according to Lavoy. He believed that without knowledge of addiction, a person with addiction would have practically no hope of any treatment method succeeding. However, without application and action, education alone would accomplish nothing. He hoped that Robbins and the manuscript could provide the knowledge and evoke motivation in, a significant number of those in need.

He rifled through his papers. *Ah yes, addiction begins with a quick reward. Often this will be an instant gratification. For example, a puff of crack or nicotine is inhaled to the lungs and is absorbed into the blood. It then goes to the heart's left atrium then ventricle and on to the brain in less than two seconds. Very few medicines, except for the anti-asthma inhaler, can work so immediately. There is so much people can learn to help them understand why they're addicted and how to overcome it.*

The next couple of hours evaporated as Lavoy scanned some of the notes and anecdotes so as to absorb them, while merely skimming others. It was obvious that some of the data would not be consistent with today's knowledge, so research would be necessary. Probably more had been written on smoking than any other topic, except maybe God. Yet not all had been written, and many had not yet read or heard, much less responded to, the need and call to quit for good.

Lavoy began an arduous task of developing a new way to conceptualize addiction and a new paradigm for addressing it. He knew there was a need for a better way for people to learn about and understand the affliction of addiction and the treatment approach. The work should certainly not be in competition with AA's twelve-step program, which is the gold standard self-help program that has proved successful for countless alcohol addicts, yet with an estimated success rate of only thirty-five percent. This would be another treatment approach for those still seeking an alternative or augmenting avenue to successful abstinence.

Lavoy thought, *Wouldn't it be wonderful if some treatment method could be as instant a cure as crack can be instantly addictive?* But that technique is still awaiting discovery. Little did he know that Samuel Robbins would bring him one such "cure" on his very next visit.

CHAPTER 5

The Right Stand

"I'VE GOT A new cure for smoking to tell you about," Robbins greeted Lavoy at their next meeting. He continued, "Last week, I visited an old college friend down in Montgomery. It worked out for me to play eighteen holes with him as a stand-in with his foursome. One of the players was a no-nonsense surgeon who took his game, life, and politics seriously. I did my usual thing of bringing up smoking and commented that none of the four were smoking. Further, I commented that it was a blight on humanity and it had taken me several attempts before I conquered it; then, like so many others, a few years later developed cancer.

"The surgeon took the opportunity to tell me his story of how he quit only once and for good. It intrigued me. He read an article in the newspaper that the Gideons would be holding an open meeting at a local facility on an upcoming Saturday afternoon. He said he had always harbored a curiosity about who the Gideons were, knowing nothing about them except that they placed Bibles in hotel rooms. Deciding that this would be a good opportunity to find out, he made arrangements and went to the meeting. He had been a heavy smoker for twenty-five years. He always had one last cigarette before going into any meeting. He approached the entrance still smoking his pre-meeting cigarette. A Gideon greeter reached out and took the cigarette from the surgeon's hand; and looking him in the eye said simply, 'You won't be needing this anymore.'

"He said the memory of that moment was indelibly burned into his mind with raging anger -- that this man or anyone would dare do this to him. He said what happened was the oddest thing. He went in and took his seat and stayed for the entire meeting, but he remembers not one word spoken or anything that happened inside the building, only the incident that occurred prior to his entering the meeting. He remained furious for hours. No one would presume to tell him what to do or what he would need or not need, and certainly would not risk being subjected to his practiced and perfected vitriolic retribution for crossing him, let alone touching him or taking something from him. But his only visible response had been turning a deep beet red. Looking back, he figures he was mighty lucky that he didn't have a stroke. Beyond that, he cannot explain what happened, but he never smoked again. He swears he never had an interest in picking up another cigarette. He did comment that he figured maybe God had tricked him that day. I tried, but in vain, to draw him out on that point, but he firmly demurred. Maybe we should make the Gideons part of our war on addictions. Everybody wants an instant cure."

"Admittedly, Sam, that's one of the best anecdotal success stories that I've ever heard. While we accept miracles gladly, we do look for logical physical and psychological explanations. In the surgeon's case, what we see is the ultimate engagement of the emotion linked directly to the phrase, 'You won't be needing this anymore.' Remember our previous discussions about thoughts having power only through the engagement of the emotion? Addiction can sometimes happen as quickly as his disappeared. If a person experiences such emotional excitement or joy on an initial contact, say for example with crack, one may be instantly addicted. Generally, it builds up with these pleasant sensations adding on top of each other until finally they cause the addiction. What we see in the surgeon is the equivalent of a total opposite force, or a reaction formation, where everything he could muster was drawn up and sustained for -- what, an hour or more? That is an incredible power play. It determined his whole mindset for possibly days or weeks to come, by which time his withdrawal symptoms had been abated with his intense emotions.

"Think about it this way. Imprinting on the mind or brain is analogous to branding the skin of cattle. You see, the emotional energy is equivalent to the branding iron. The more emotional energy or the more heat in the branding iron, the more deep and permanent will be the resulting effect -- either on the skin or on the imprint in the mind. Quick, intense, or very intense pleasure or displeasure either pulls us in or pushes us away. But unless it was a true miracle, the addiction would be lifelong; it would always be there waiting for his weak moment to have just one little slip, one more puff, one more cigarette. That's all it would have taken to rekindle the full force of the addictive monster within him. He apparently got a hardwired program never to try it again. For most of us, the addictive craving is always lurking beneath the surface, waiting for a weak moment to pounce and recapture us by seducing us to have just one more go at it. Alcoholics have known that for years and have paraphrased that knowledge by saying, 'one drink away from being a drunk.'"

"Or one more cigarette," Sam extrapolated.

"Or, for that matter, one more anything might undo the miracle."

"That's sad," Sam spoke his thought.

"In the medical field, most of us consider addiction a disease. We treat it with the medical model. I will be teaching you the fundamental aspects. You also need to know that some consider addiction as a spiritual problem. Ideally, in my opinion, treatment should blend the two approaches. Most programs are one or the other. One spiritually based program that impresses me is the Foundry at Bessemer, Alabama. They do a lot of things right. I like them keeping people a year and having them work to pay their keep. They restore a person's self worth to know they are worthy of living a clean and wholesome life. Addiction is a chronic incurable condition. The good news is that it can be arrested and even reversed. However, the biophysiological changes never revert to their original base line. The drive to continue the addictive substance or behavior never quits, even if it is not conscious. Many addicts talk of their addiction dreams, often years after their last indulgence. One use totally revitalizes the addiction.

"A recovering addict has to be ever vigilant to avoid the substance. For example, alcoholics must avoid medicine, even cough syrup, that contains alcohol. One has to especially avoid allowing a doctor to give them narcotics for pain."

Sam responded, "That makes good sense. You know, Doc, if I'm going to give talks at schools, and civic organizations, etc., I figure it might help to sprinkle in some interesting Alabama historical notes. While I was in Montgomery, I visited the Alabama Department of Archives and History. I had no idea we are so rich in history and so much is preserved. Montgomery, you know, was not the first capital of Alabama, but it was the first capital of the Confederacy. Jefferson Davis and his family lived there in the first 'White House of the Confederacy,' which is preserved. Then over time, Alabama swung its pendulum 180 degrees to become the prime state for the Civil Rights movement. Have you ever visited the Maya Lin beautiful black granite Civil Rights memorial that recognizes the forty martyrs to the cause, proclaiming Alabama's pride in being the lynchpin state to bring about racial equality? Alabama's stubbornness cost us dearly in lives and media image. Perhaps history will recognize the importance of Alabama in the seismic cultural and political transformation born here."

"Great thinking and good points, Sam. Did you ever think about the fact that Alabama has been first in so many things? Even space, including extraterrestrial flight to the moon." Lavoy added, "Some of our symbolism is almost too supernatural to recognize or understand. Take, for instance, Governor George Wallace. He famously stood in the doorway at the University of Alabama in Tuscaloosa to block integration. Then during his Presidential campaign, a would-be assassin managed to shoot him at close range. He did not lose his life, but what did he lose? His ability to stand, which was a symbol for the world to see, if they had the inner sight to see. Apparently, Governor Wallace saw it for himself, as he would later both privately and publicly make genuine amends to the black race, actually proclaiming the *right stand*.

"Well, next time I have some more interesting ideas to discuss with you regarding addiction."

CHAPTER 6

Anagram

SAM, NOW FOUR weeks into treatment, immediately answered Lavoy's as yet unspoken, but predictable greeting. "I feel great. I'm ready to get off this medicine." He was, in that respect, no different from the majority of patients. As soon as they feel better, they equate it to being cured and believe they are ready to discontinue their medication.

"That's great, I'm glad that you're doing well," Lavoy complimented. "If you had come to me with hunger and malnutrition, then after four weeks of food and nutritional stabilization would you say that you were well and ready to get off food? In each scenario, once you are stabilized, you must be maintained with food or medicine to continue a healthy balance of nutrition or chemicals. Food, of course, you will need for life. Antidepressants you may or you may not. If your depression turns out to be situationally precipitated or caused by your illness and consequent stresses and lifestyle, you may indeed recover completely and be able to function normally and healthily without medicines, but it would be a mistake to prematurely risk that stability by discontinuing your medication before we can be sure. There is a possibility that you may have an underlying bipolar disorder, given your family history, and this could have precipitated a bipolar episode of depression or mania. In that case, you would likely need to be on medication for life. As we follow you longer and know you better, we will be better able to discern definitively which type of depression you have."

"Okay, you're the doc. I think I see what you mean. I'll try to be more patient. I do feel good. My wife says I'm better than at any time since my cancer diagnosis. I feel normal."

After assessing that Sam's mood was normal and not manic, Lavoy relaxed and the two of them settled into discussions on the "war on addiction."

"I promised to have something interesting for you this time. Let me show you an anagram that I've been working on. It's a succinct synopsis of accepting, understanding, and treating addiction."

"That's cool. Is it easy?"

"To learn, yes. To accomplish is for the individual to say; but it is a fantastic tool, a guide, and platform for us to use." Lavoy handed Sam his typed notes, including a brief and an expanded version. "Let me know what you think. I will value your opinion."

War on Addiction

Admit addiction
Declare freedom from addiction
Declare commitment to healthy body, soul, work, and relationships
Imagine a healthy lifestyle without addictive substances
Commit to continual self-education about addiction
Teach others all you can about addiction
Involve a buddy
Own up to personal responsibilities and shortcomings
Never let your guard down

War on Addiction

Admit addiction – This applies to any and all addictions, and that's the beauty of this anagram.
Declare freedom from addiction – As with all freedom, it must be

constantly defended and won over and over again. The declaration should be your personal *war on addiction*, but everyone together can also make it a global effort.

Declare commitment to healthy body, soul, work, and relationships – You must have a healthy body to function well day to day and to fight any battles or wars. When your soul or spirit is happy, it is easier to win personal battles. When you dedicate yourself to fostering a healthy work environment, you're making a major effort in an extremely important segment of your life. Relationship health is a place to derive continual happiness and unequaled support. Give it everything you have.

Imagine a healthy lifestyle without addictive substances – It should be easy to envision yourself being carefree and untethered from the addictive substance. Often people continue to look backward; and rather than feeling the joys of the future opportunities they mistakenly reach back for the temporary "fixes" of the past.

Commit to continued self-education about addiction – The more you learn, the better prepared you will be to win your battles with addiction. The more you learn, the more you can help others. As with anything worthwhile, a lifetime of learning will not exhaust the information available to learn.

Teach others all you can about addiction – As you repeat what you know for others, you are reinforcing the knowledge to yourself, but you are simultaneously imparting it to others who need it.

Involve a buddy – This is important. It is someone for whom you give of yourself, but it is also someone from whom you receive in times of personal crisis or needs. Choose someone compatible.

Own up to personal responsibilities and shortcomings – Until one is able to recognize and admit their own shortcomings, they're not being honest with themselves. Until one accepts the responsibilities that should be their own, they're not being equitable or fair.

Never let your guard down – You must always have an ironclad defense, for there are inevitable urges and impulses that will assail you by all means possible. These will come at your weakest and most needy moments. Avoid persons, places, and situations that are opportunistic for addictive substance and behavior.

"That's nice, Doc. It's like making the addiction fight itself. I like that. It also gives bullet points that are easy to remember and talk from."

"Excellent observation. Each one can be discussed at length depending on the situation, how much the discussant knows, and how much time and interest the audience allows. You will research and explore each point as we develop our program, then you will have it all organized."

"Okay, you're planning another blue book. Will it compete with AA?"

"No, not at all. The blue book is a good book. I'll stick to the novel format. Real life struggles that show how some win and others lose the struggle."

Lavoy offered a personal observation regarding AA. "Sam, AA invokes an important and profound point that we should not ignore. It speaks of an addict's 'powerlessness' over addiction; then it mentions our spiritual need for a higher power. I see that as a double entendre or a paradox. Notice while it leaves wanting those who would prefer their chosen spiritual path be recognized, it nevertheless satisfies all who are spiritually grounded and need to see an acknowledgment of the importance and healing power of the spiritual realm. One can infer that the power of God is **the**, or at least **a**, treatment for addiction. However, the program then offers the secular steps to overcome addiction. Is the choice left to the addict, or is the directive more imperative that we should accept the dual treatment approach to addiction? We also see that the word 'spiritual' is used in its most broad form, leaving further personal interpretation. For me, it strongly persuades me that spiritual health is necessary to be free of addiction."

"Addiction's rough stuff, Doc. Do you intend to be open and honest in the book? Hey, how do I turn out? Will I be in your book?"

"If you like, but not by name. Suppose you're the lead character.

How do you want to turn out? For all we know, how you feel about that answer could be the single most important element affecting your outcome."

"Excellent point. And I do have that grandson to think about, you know."

"How old is your grandson? Do the two of you get together often?"

"After the cancer, we sure do. Getting face to face with mortality gives one a better perspective on living; and, for that matter, teaching life. I want him to know life and how to enjoy it. He is a fine five-year-old boy."

"That brush with cancer might make you a philosopher, Sam."

"No, I don't think so. It's just that I never before gave any thought to my life ending. For a while there, I was dwelling on it pretty hard. That just sucked all the joy out of living."

"I'm glad you've rebounded and are enjoying life and living. Keep it up. Let's get together Wednesday for lunch and keep this project going. Here, take this with you. It's a typed account of the way that I was able to quit smoking. I promised I would share it with you. Here it is."

"Thanks, I'll read it tonight," Sam promised.

CHAPTER 7

Lavoy's Vignette

FIRST OF ALL, it was not easy. I required three separate attempts, each years apart.

March 15, 1972. I was only three and a half months short of finishing my psychiatry residency and starting private practice. I was having lunch with a fellow resident and his wife. The three of us were discussing the need to quit smoking. Each of us had tried previously. I had at that time been smoking since 1953, essentially nineteen years.

My first attempt to quit was in 1960. After I had been without a cigarette or any tobacco for nine months, I was tempted one night at a party. I was feeling good, having fun, and felt invincible. And surely what harm would it be to just have one? Having that one cigarette brought back a more powerful craving for more cigarettes than I had ever previously experienced. I probably smoked a whole pack before that night was over.

Once again I quit in 1963, when I graduated from medical school, thinking I really should quit. By then we knew there were dangers to your health from smoking. There was a huge national educational program touting that 100,000 doctors had quit smoking. Did they know something that you didn't? After quitting for an entire year that time, I felt quite sure that I would be able to handle just one. The same powerful addiction proved me wrong and I smoked again until this lunch on March 15, 1972.

My friends had similar experiences. Being students we were, of course, nearly broke. So the three of us bet each other that for $100 each of us could be the one to not smoke. So, whichever person smoked first would owe the other two $100 each. I knew that I couldn't afford $100, let alone $200. The other two were a married couple. So I had to be the one not smoking. Two days after we made that bet, I learned that their child had been seriously injured in an accident. We simply never mentioned smoking to each other again. But being 48 hours without a cigarette and very desirous to never smoke again, and not wanting to enter a psychiatric practice where my patients could see me addicted to a cigarette, I made up my mind to never smoke again. And I haven't. Was it uncomfortable? Sure. Was it an addiction? Positively. Is the addiction still present? Of course it is. One year after I quit smoking, I dreamed one night of smoking a foot-long, very satisfying cigarette. Furthermore, twelve years after quitting, I had a bout with mono that lasted for several weeks. I repeatedly dreamed that I was smoking cigarettes. It subsided after I awoke during one of the dreams, realizing that I had been dreaming repeatedly. You must remember that addiction will try to find a way back into your life and it will pick your weakest moments and your weakest areas. It will use the cleverest of tactics. Some examples are: "For old times' sake; just this once; it will make you feel better; it will show that you have mastered it; no one has to know; you will be proud to know that after abstaining so long you can handle it now; new treatments and techniques have improved treatment; the newer cigarettes aren't as dangerous." Your own mind will invent its own clever deceptions, neatly tied into your own interests, trying every trick to satisfy the lingering *permanent* addictive craving.

At their next meeting, Sam thanked Dr. Lavoy for sharing the story of his personal battle with smoking addiction. He added, "You just needed something to get you started. Why is it such a problem for us to quit?"

"Sam, the first day I met you that question was personal. You wanted to know why you smoked all those years. Smoking addiction is very complicated. Remember, nicotine is a powerful brain stimulant. When one inhales the smoke of a cigarette or a more powerful cigar, the nicotine is filtered out by the lungs. It goes into the blood then the heart then quickly to the brain. That is about the quickest reward one can get and it is powerful.

"Next the blood circulates through the body. When it goes through the liver it stimulates the liver to release glycogen into the bloodstream. That is essentially the immediate usable form of sugar; think of it as an intravenous drip of honey. At that time one gets a second and longer-lasting pleasant sensation. After regular exposure to nicotine, the brain and body insist on more of it, more frequently; that is addiction. When the body and brain can't get the nicotine, they then begin to rebel and demand it. That means physical dependency and withdrawal, a very uncomfortable condition. In fact, one can die in withdrawal from alcohol and from barbiturates as well. Some pain medicines contain barbiturates and opiates in combination. These are highly addictive and very dangerous.

"In addition to all the foregoing, one simply gets in the habit of doing things. For example, if one wears a nicotine patch and is not in withdrawal, he will still habitually reach for his cigarette. Furthermore, one will use the cigarette socially, perhaps as a conversation opener or even at times as a barrier, knowing that it will keep someone away or at a safer distance. So you can see, Sam, overcoming addiction is not a simple matter. It is a multifaceted illness. We will discuss other fascinating aspects of addiction later."

"I had no idea," said Sam.

"Most people don't," replied Lavoy.

Sam was curious about another topic. "Doc," Sam asked, "I've heard that hypnosis is a good way to quit smoking. Is there anything to that or is that wishful thinking?"

"Actually, Sam, hypnosis is a very good way to quit smoking. It's also used quite effectively to help people lose weight, get a good night's sleep, and to lower anxiety and blood pressure through relaxation techniques. The one thing you want to be careful of is that you have a trained and qualified person doing the hypnosis. I and other hypnotists have been able to use this technique successfully to block nausea for those who are having nausea from chemotherapy. It is also effective in blocking pain, but one would have to be careful not to block pain that might be signaling a pathology that needs to be recognized. Untrained hypnotists may remove one bad habit only to have it substituted with a worse problem. If you remove someone's coping technique and they can't cope further, you're inviting more trouble. Hypnosis sometimes is used to recover buried information. One must remember that it is buried for a reason and if it is forced to the surface without proper protective measures, one might cause a full-blown psychotic episode. Hypnosis is a unique, mystifying, and powerful tool.

"Let me tell you a funny -- but sad -- story about smoking. Once a patient came to see me for hypnosis to stop smoking. She was in her sixties. I asked her why she had decided to come for hypnosis after smoking all those years. She told me that she had seen her pulmonologist and he told her that if she did not stop smoking she would be dead in six months. Then she added, 'And Doctor, it's been four months.' I explored with her the knowledge of cigarettes being bad for her and the knowledge that they can cause death. Then she realized that her smoking was a way of slowly getting out of a life that she was not enjoying.

"By the way, Sam, there's another interesting addiction that needs discussion -- relationship addictions, the roots of which we know are formed in the first seven years of life. Of course, there are other avenues of treatment for that also, such as couples or marriage counseling. Relationship addiction is actually one of the more intriguing addictions. It is often mentioned as co-dependency, perhaps better understood as the need to be in a relationship even if abusive or neglectful. Some display symptoms of what is colloquially termed a love-hate relationship. This is a *folie à deux*, which is an illness shared by two people, though we do not find it so categorized in the

DSM-IV-R [Diagnostic and Statistical Manual Fourth Edition Revised]. Intense anger or pleasure in these relationships may trigger the release of endorphins. Certainly, the pleasure center is involved. In these relationships, pleasurable sensations often depend more on endorphin highs than true happiness. The paucity of outside pleasure is often a handicap in one's ability to avoid turning to drugs. Relationship addiction requires expert treatment, preferably before drugs compound the problem, making it a dual addiction. Usually treatment comes after one spouse has been through a detox program.

"There is a recognized psychiatric syndrome classified as poly-substance abuse. Obviously, it means one's abusing or being addicted to more than one substance of abuse, usually alcohol and marijuana or opiates or benzodiazepine tranquilizers or any combination of these. A significant number of couples are in addictive relationships without consciously realizing it. Yet sensing its impropriety, they purposefully don't tell their physician or counselor. A significant number are poly-substance abusers.

"For example, the relationship above might be one depending on, say, three cups of coffee to get started and tranquilizers to tolerate the daily encounters with a partner. The individual might even smoke, especially at strategic moments, and may use alcohol to survive the evening and get to sleep. Most likely, that person is being treated for *nervousness* or *anxiety* or even just *stress*.

"We should be considering the term poly-addictive syndrome as well as poly-substance abuse. We generally do not think of relationship difficulties, or coffee abuse, running, eating, or buying excessive shoes as addictive, but for some they are addictions and we ignore them and their consequences at our peril.

"We need to see, know, and understand the common components and dangers of addiction. We must recognize it in ourselves and in others. It is our responsibility to fight it for ourselves and others."

CHAPTER **8**

A Broad View

WEDNESDAY AT NOON Sam had already been waiting patiently in Dr. Lavoy's waiting room for five minutes. Sam was feeling more like himself now – even rejuvenated. He was in his sixth month of treatment for his depression. He had been able to convince Dr. Lavoy that he could function without the medication as he was participating in satisfying activities to combat any lingering depression. He was no longer seeing Dr. Lavoy as a patient and had come prepared for this first official single-purpose meeting to strategize their mission, now named "War on Addiction." He had loaded his briefcase with items enthusiastically accumulated. He collected any information of even the remotest possible use. Surely everything was worth keeping. There were newspaper articles, magazine articles, testimonials, advertisements for various smoking materials, as well as alcohol products. There were even advertisements for smoking cessation and alcohol rehabilitation programs. He had a smug feeling that Dr. Lavoy was going to be impressed with his collection.

It was almost 12:30 by the time Lavoy summoned Sam, who easily perceived Lavoy's enthusiasm for the meeting. Sam quickly forgot about the wait time. He had spent the time talking to one of Lavoy's patients before settling into reading one of the magazines and collecting another article for his briefcase.

Dr. Lavoy had sandwiches brought in for the convenience of being able to spread their information out on the conference table. This war on addiction was going to need their full attention. Lavoy had finally found someone he believed to be a most promising motivational speaker to make a difference in the treatment of addiction. He saw in Sam an intelligent convert with evangelical enthusiasm and a believable persona. His innate ability and enthusiasm would go far in promoting the cause.

Both were visibly excited to see how much material the other had brought to the table. Sam was eager to show off his collected materials, now neatly organized into sources, and listed on index cards by subject. Unconsciously showing his eagerness to begin speaking, Sam first showed a prepared list of clubs, organizations, churches, and schools where he wanted to give talks and tell of the dangers of smoking. He said that he had a great idea. He was going to prepare a poster that he would display. It would show him in his previous healthy, smiling, gregarious state and then contrast this with a picture of a cancerous lung. Then he would ask the question, "Was it worth it?" He would answer himself, "No, it wasn't, but I was ignorant of the consequences and stupid to risk it. The only question that remains is: now that you are informed of the risk, will you be stupid? As I was, even after learning the dangers?"

"Sam, you're going to be great at this."

"That anagram really made me think. It is my responsibility not just to stay free, but to learn all I can and pass it forward to everyone who will listen. Who knows how little we know **until** we learn what we didn't know?"

"That's close to a Yogism, Sam. Take a look at this array of scientific papers that I've been collecting these past thirty years. The level of knowledge on addiction, like most everything, has grown almost exponentially. We want to remember that the time is right for the war on addiction – all types, so let's not limit ourselves to one aspect. We are learning the commonalities between the various types of addiction. In fact, next week I want to outline the known forms of addiction. I'll take that as my assignment."

"And maybe I can think of more 'grabbers' for my audiences."

"That would be good, Sam. You might even want to join Toastmasters, not that I think you need it."

"I can take a hint."

"We just need to do everything possible to do this right. Just look at these statistics of US citizens," Lavoy offered, showing Sam his chart.

- One out of four is a current smoker.
- One out of four is an ex-smoker.
- One out of two people is or has been a smoker.
- Nearly one out of two smokers die of a smoking-related disease – cancer, chronic obstructive lung disease, heart and blood vessel disease, peptic ulcers, other gastric diseases, fetal and maternal complication, and so on.
- One out of five deaths overall is smoking-related.
- One out of two smokers started before fifteen years of age. "We have to get to them early, Sam," Lavoy remarked.
- One out of three smokers tries every year to quit. Ninety percent try on their own with no professional help.
- One out of three quitters has abstinence of less than two days.
- Only one out of two smoking addicts who tries is able to eventually quit, even after multiple attempts.
- Tobacco-related deaths are often agonizing and slow.

Sam responded, "One half of smokers started before they were fifteen years old? I'm going to talk to Brian again and often. I hadn't thought it important to start talking to them at such a young age."

"Speaking of pictures, Sam, I want to point out something to you. In the list of illnesses mentioned earlier, the largest organ of the body is affected tremendously, yet is rarely mentioned, just as it was left off that list. I'm talking about the skin. We need to find some pictures of same-age people – those who smoke and don't, men and women.

What you will see is that those who are chronic smokers have skin much different from those who never smoked. Often, they are going to be noticeably different. Everything else being equal, you will see that the non-smoker generally has soft, pliable, colorful, healthy-appearing skin, usually with the person smiling. On the other hand, smokers will generally appear to have leathery, rough, wrinkled, yellowish, unhealthy skin, on people who are not smiling. Precisely because we are so emotionally charged by our image, such photographs will likely have a profound impact on viewers. My hope is that once the war on addiction becomes known that we will have pairs of identical twins – one who smoked and one who didn't – send us their pictures so that we can see the drastic differences. It should be very dramatic when we know the DNA was the same. It would be analogous to an instant before and after photograph. That would really help the war on addiction effort."

"I bet we'll find them," Sam offered confidently.

CHAPTER 9

Addiction Monster

DR. LAVOY AND Sam had decided on bi-weekly meetings, schedules permitting. At their next meeting, they again spread their materials out on the conference table, exhibiting childlike enthusiasm, but also mature, seasoned organization.

Lavoy began by saying that initially he had found some information on several of the recognized addictions. "It will be necessary for us to look at each of them for basic information. We will also need to compile a source list so that people can readily access desired information on each and all of the addictions. The more accessible and easy we make it, the better our chances and the public's chances of looking into it and getting the help they need."

Sam's eagerness showed when he turned on his recorder. While reaching for his pen and paper, he said, "I'm ready, let's hear it."

"We've already addressed a fair amount regarding the smoking addiction, but a little repetition won't hurt us.

"In the US, over seventy million people use some form of tobacco in order to get nicotine. Roughly sixty percent of those are male and forty percent female. Nicotine produces physical dependence and physical withdrawal symptoms. Caffeine is the most prevalently used of all the addictive substances. It is obtained through the use of coffee, tea, cocoa, chocolate, and tablets. It is regularly used by approximately eighty-five percent of the US population. It produces physical dependence and physical withdrawal symptoms.

"Alcohol is used by more than two hundred million people, or two-thirds of the US population. Close to ten percent of the population (thirty million) are problem drinkers; many are addicted and/or dependent. It produces physical dependence and physical withdrawal symptoms, including delirium tremens (commonly called DTs). This is a life-threatening event, and many people died in DTs before modern detoxification techniques. Over ten thousand per day try alcohol for the first time. These are staggering numbers.

"Drugs, illegal as well as prescription, invade and addict thousands of individuals daily, totaling around four million people in the US. Fresh addicts replenish the void left by those who die daily from overdose, both accidental and intentional, and other related causes including motor vehicle accidents, health related problems, and crime associated deaths. These include the opioids -- many by prescription -- but also the various street preparations. Also, angel dust or PCP (phencyclidine), LSD (lysergic acid), GBH (gaba-rohypnol), and marijuana are included in this class. At any given time roughly one out of five addicts is in some form of treatment."

"I'm getting the message, Doc. It's not just smoking and smokers. This addiction monster is like a transformer right out of horror movies, except it's maniacally and powerfully real. It takes multiple forms, paths, and opportunities to find our hedonistic and fun-loving vulnerabilities."

"That's right, Sam. Its easiest and most frequent entrance is through the youthful gateway, drugs introduced through peer pressure. Peer acceptance is a powerful motivator. And when initiation seems to be both innocuous and rewarding, the unwitting victim thinks 'no big deal.' Furthermore, the behavior usually continues undetected until the impulse for pleasure becomes physically undeniable or dependence has developed. The timing is usually during the individual's experimental efforts to learn who he or she is or when they are attempting to move beyond being the parent's child protégé. Too many parents are woefully uneducated about this constant threat to family tranquility. They must first become educated so as to render proper guidance and education to their children. One cannot teach their children things about which they themselves are ignorant; they can, however, set a good example even without knowledge or understanding."

"That's our job, right, Doc?"

"It's an effort that we are joining. We want to make a difference. Sam, to whatever extent we can be leaders in what must be an all out committed effort or *war on addiction*, we should accept the challenge. Peer pressure is important at any age, but the monster has other means of getting its hook into us. Doctors prescribe addictive drugs to help relieve anxiety or pain. Pushers find ways to get people to try addictive substances. Often a 'friend' will make the introduction and suggestion to try it with them. Not infrequently, there is an unexpected feeling of euphoria. Some are instantly hooked. 'Hey, where has this been all my life?' Others take longer, but the hook is nevertheless slowly and insidiously set."

"That's the way it happened to me. You sure have gotten my adrenaline pumping. I see those kids out there on the athletic teams, in the classrooms, and on the streets. I don't want to let even one be ignorant of what dangers the addiction monster is hiding from them behind that beguiling façade, offering them what appears to be nothing but pleasure, fun, and frivolity."

"There are many subtle ways the addiction monster eases its hook into us, Sam," Lavoy shared his knowledge. "Alcohol, tranquilizers, and narcotics are all sedatives to us, but they play a cruel and mean trick on us. They disinhibit us. We think we have been stimulated. Our pleasure receptors are stimulated and simultaneously we are tranquilized. Think about it: a pill or a drink transforms someone from being bored or moody to being tranquil and happy. That is mighty powerful.

"As we develop in childhood we acquire social graces and societal rules. These inhibit us from saying and doing things we might otherwise do for our personal gratification. When these addictive

substances disinhibit us, we feel free to say and do personally gratifying things, even at the expense of others. Join this disinhibited feeling
with a tranquil, happy feeling -- and before you catch on, the powerful monster has his hook in you, yet cleverly is making you feel
deliriously tranquil, happy, and powerful yourself."

Sam said, "That gives me a better understanding of being power-
less over addiction." He continued, "I see that we have to not only
role model, but teach the young children never to start with addictive
substances -- and we must be doubly vigilant teaching and treating
those already walking the addiction path. How do you propose we
go about this task?"

"If there's anyone who will be able to convince people to listen,
surely it has to be you, Sam. It does help to have a workable plan. I
have written one out for you. Let's go over it. Once you go through it,
you will see that it is easily remembered.

"To help someone quit smoking or any addiction, remember
METEL. It is up to each of us to tell addicts how to quit. It is me telling you; everyone must pass it on. I suggest offering printed cards
such as this," handing Sam a pre-printed card. "Perhaps they could
be laminated."

M – First, motivate.
E – Second, educate.
T – Third, teach techniques to quit.
E – Fourth, endure.
L – Fifth, love self better than cigarettes, drugs, alcohol, etc.

Motivate: There are positive and negative motivations. To motivate
someone, you must positively promote the benefits of not smoking
or drinking, etc. The following points should be separately discussed
with individuals with whom you talk.

• You live years longer.
• You are more likely to receive affection.

- You are more productive.
- You are more likely to be promoted.
- You save a ton of money.
- You are less likely to have an accident.
- You won't get smoker's cough.
- You never have to go out at night to find a cigarette.
- You avoid those nasty stares.
- Your wardrobe doesn't smell like tobacco.
- You don't need to interrupt what you are doing to get your next fix.
- You will be unbelievably healthier and happier.
- You will attract more friends.
- You will be more credible.
- You will be respected more.

Then you should continue the motivation by elaborating the negatives.

- You die years younger.
- You smell like stale tobacco.
- People avoid you when you smoke and when you smell like smoke.
- You drastically increase your risk of lung cancer, heart attack, stroke, emphysema, and much, much more.
- You miss out on some invitations.
- You spend tons of money on short term stimulation while investing heavily in long term misery.
- You are less productive.
- You're less likely to be promoted.
- You are much more susceptible to infection including bronchitis, pneumonia, sinusitis, and even gastritis.
- Cognitively, you are less alert even when you are craving a fix.
- You could have defective sperm or eggs.
- The list is too long to print here.

After Sam had gone over these points, Lavoy continued, "Education is the second point, Sam. People must be educated about addiction, and that will be the core message we will deliver in our meetings and our talks. They need to know how people become addicted, especially since no one wants to be addicted and even deny it when they, in fact, are addicted. They need to know what addiction is and why it is so difficult to overcome. They need to understand why and how addiction is permanent.

"It is very important that they realize the likelihood of addicts having a co-morbid illness. In fact, often the discomfort they experience from an underlying illness is one of the risk factors that makes them an easy target for addiction. In treatment, it is imperative that both the addiction and the co-morbid illness are treated. If either one is untreated, one's vulnerability is greatly increased.

"For most, quitting will not be a simple decision, but they will often say, 'I'll just stop smoking.' This third step is up to you, me, and the treatment programs. We must teach others how to quit. While all addictions have much in common, each will have individual differences. Smoking is a powerful and complicated addiction. Understanding the intricacies of a smoker's addiction and the necessary things to know and overcome, as well as the technique used, is immensely helpful to the addict attempting to quit smoking, but quite instructive to anyone struggling with most any addiction.

"Most smokers know that they get an immediate reward of pleasure with the first drag off a cigarette. Most are clueless as to all that goes into the overall conversion to addiction. This is important information that they should know. Nicotine is a powerful stimulant to the brain's dopamine (feel good) system. The cigarette provides many puffs, saturating the dopamine system. This is a reason people with mental illnesses such as schizophrenia smoke excessively.

"It takes about four hours for the effect of nicotine to wear off enough to truly need another infusion. Also, nicotine circulates to the liver and releases glycogen. This sugar-like substance makes us feel good. We have a two-punch reward. The dopamine receptors become so accustomed to being powerfully and regularly stimulated that they become sluggish without nicotine. This is an opposite feeling, therefore we feel bad. The body begins to withdraw with feelings of nervousness, perspiring, rapid pulse, and restlessness. We crave the nicotine fiercely. If you have experienced withdrawal, you can remember the stress.

"There is also a strong habit component. We habitually reach for the cigarette at specific times or social cues or stress. Abstainers talk of reaching for cigarettes long after they were discarded. Habits can be difficult to break. It is uncomfortable and stressful to deny a habit.

"Additionally, there are convenient benefits. It's a good excuse to take a break from work. It's an easy barrier to put between yourself and someone you would rather not be close to at the moment. When you give up your cigarettes, you lose one of your social tools. Any loss is yet another stressor. In fact, the chances are that if you quit smoking or drinking or drugging, you will very likely gravitate to a different circle of friends. After a person becomes educated about their addiction it will be less difficult, but certainly not easy for most people."

Lavoy gave Sam another, but shorter list summarizing the steps to walk away from smoking.

1) Give up the nicotine high
2) Give up the secondary sugar rush from glycogen
3) Go through breaking the habit
4) Give up a social tool and possibly your circle of friends

"How can you successfully accomplish all of these things?" Lavoy asked, and went on to answer his own question. "One way is cold turkey: that is tackling each component all at one time. It is the most stressful, but quickest method. Furthermore, it is the one most likely to fail and the one most often tried. The most difficult part is the nicotine addiction, so it should be the last part to address.

"The social use is the least difficult, so it should be the first to address. It takes thought and decisions about alternate ways to interact with others. If you are unable on your own, then you should seek professional counseling. Be aware that the second highest rate of success is the structured cessation programs – at least for smoking. They usually employ a scheduled nicotine reduction program with education and group sessions and/or buddy support through the acute phase. Hypnosis likely has the highest success rate.

"Usually, it is helpful to continue nicotine (but not alcohol and opiates) until the habit and social interaction stress has abated to an acceptable level. Nicotine is typically provided through gum or a patch. I don't like the patch except in hospital settings. I don't like the idea of nicotine continuing during sleep. The rate of heart attacks goes up in those with a patch if they also smoke. Gum works quicker than the patch and is used more intermittently, more similar to a smoke, unlike the steady release by the patch. The gum is powerful and should not be thoroughly chewed at one time. In fact, it can be used briefly and reused. Nicotine is the addictive substance, therefore one must guard against transferring the addiction to the gum or patch.

"It is helpful to some to place a cutout of cardboard roughly the size of a pack of cigarettes where the cigarettes were kept. They may want to put a note on it saying, 'No, you can't have just one.' They might want to add, 'Now laugh at yourself and get on with your life.' For opiates and benzodiazepines, it is much better to detox in a safe and secure facility. One's chances of success are much better if they complete a residential rehab program.

"The fourth and necessary step is the endurance of the discomfort that accompanies detoxification and withdrawal -- the cravings that likely will be strong and frequent for several weeks and linger for months or even years. People must remember that every day of endurance builds strength to endure the next one. But failure to endure dooms one's effort.

"Addicts must think better of themselves than of their cigarettes or alcohol or drug. The fifth step is when the addicts put themselves above their drug of choice. When someone is clean of the addictive substance, they should be encouraged to take stock of how much healthier they are. If they don't like themselves better or appreciate themselves more or have a better outlook, they should go for professional counseling.

"It's important to remind people that therapy or counseling is a very private and personal relationship, yet professional. If, for any reason, someone is not progressing, talk with the therapist and if the impasse is not resolved, try another therapist. Every person is a human being, worthy of salvaging – everyone should get all the help they need."

Lavoy added, "Sam, here is an opportunity that many families miss. If we could reinforce the good in people, including addicts, the positive effect might surprise us. Unfortunately, the addict's behavior is so abhorrent that we too often just attack the negative. The attention is like fertilizer on weeds. This is a real tricky balancing act for families. We can't condone or ignore the bad behavior. For this technique to work positively, it must be in tandem with motivation, education, assistance in quitting or rehab techniques, and patient endurance.

"I know this was a lot, Sam, but I hope it will help you understand addiction better -- yours, mine, and ours. If it does, it will also help you reach others who struggle with their addiction monsters. You will see as we proceed that there is much more to learn about addiction. You will find unexpected frustrations that interfere with your struggles concerning addiction. Remember, endure them all, for they are each temporary, but your goal is permanent!"

"Now that's a really good point, Doc. Thanks for writing it out."

"No problem, Sam -- eventually we will need to write all of them down."

CHAPTER 10

Marriage Matters

SAM ARRIVED HOME glowing with excitement about war on addiction. He found Kitty, making sure everything was in its proper place. Sam neglected to inquire about her day and began telling her about his and Dr. Lavoy's discussion of the several addictions and their monster-like grip over people.

"Sam, slow down, can't you talk about anything but addictions? I'm glad you have found a project. I'm happy for you. It's a noble effort. I'm proud of you for doing it and I see how much time you devote to studying. I know it will pay off and do some good. I hope lots of people will benefit. I'm sure Brian will."

Let's see, Sam reasoned, *I'm to slow down. That means I'm to get out of myself and listen to her. Then there's praise and recognition, proving that she's aware of me and approves what I'm doing. Now, there has to be a "but," so I better be listening carefully.*

Kitty continued, unaware that Sam had tuned in quicker and more intently than she expected. "It's just that you are so busy and so focused, you don't have time for me. I'm not *me* to you anymore. You didn't even say 'hello' or 'hi, honey.' I'm just a pair of ears. I need to know that I matter, Sam. I don't feel I'm a part of you anymore."

It was a bull's-eye hit. At times like this, he really needed a smoke. Sam felt the full impact. *It wasn't just today. It's me. At first it was my work, but she was busy with the house and Peggy and didn't com-*

plain. Then it was community and church activities and always more work. Of course, she was also busy and rarely complained. Then it was my cancer. Naturally, she wouldn't complain. Now it's warring against addiction. I'm out to cure the world. I'm ignoring and not rewarding my best support.

What was Kitty not saying that I should be hearing loud and clear? Sam invented her unspoken grievances. *"Am I just a domestic partner here to clean and cook? I thought this was retirement. Aren't we going to enjoy togetherness, travel, entertaining, eating out, movies, etc.? Where are my cards and flowers and sweet notes? Do I not merit them anymore?"*

Sam even doubted that Kitty had actually put those grim words to the disappointment and frustration she was feeling. He desperately hoped not. Kitty had exhibited so much joy for him, recovering from surgery and now from depression, that he had unfortunately overlooked her needs and all the energy she had necessarily expended on his behalf. It was as if he was regaining his health by draining hers. Feeling all too guilty and insensitive, he focused one hundred percent on demonstrating love, repentance, asking forgiveness, and promising renewed devotion and appreciation. He vowed to "make her happy."

"My dear sweet Kitty," Sam began, wishing that he had time to write out a proper confession and promise. "What a fool I've been. I've worked hard and taken too much credit. You've worked harder and without the credit. You've sustained me with love, food, encouragement, praise, home, a child, consultation, and when needed, consolations. You mustered the energy necessary to get me through the surgery and the depression. I got well and refocused and have unwittingly ignored your needs, all the while basking stupidly in your pleasure of my wellness. I see my error. I sincerely apologize. I ask your forgiveness because I need it. I promise it won't happen again. Help me to know how to make it up to you. I'll do whatever is in my power."

Kitty had tried several times to interrupt Sam, but he had quieted her each time with his finger. He had to say his piece.

"Sam, my sweet darling, you have to know how much I love you. You have overanalyzed my words and my feelings. I don't feel en-slaved. I am blessed, Sam. We are a team. You've done your part and I've done mine. At times I know I have been inadequate for your needs and I've felt guilty during my moments of doubt, but you haven't complained or even mentioned them. We both know that marriage is a 'give and take.' Those that don't know that are the ones that fail. I cannot presume that you need any forgiveness unless you feel that I also need forgiveness. If so," at this point Kitty was putting her arms around Sam's neck, "I hope this kiss is the yes that you want."

"Oh, it's all I need, my love." Sam gave back a kiss he had almost forgotten that he had. All their problems dissolved as they remem-bered they had the house to themselves. Ecstasy reunited Sam and Kitty as they rekindled passion and joys closed down by fighting his illnesses.

CHAPTER 11

The Day After

THE FOLLOWING MORNING as Kitty cooked Sam's favorite breakfast of scrambled eggs, crisp fried bacon, southern fluffy biscuits, cheese grits, and fruit, Sam sat contentedly reading the morning paper. This day, more than most of the recent past, he paused to offer her an affectionate glance while hoping to catch a glimpse of her bright eyes and smile. He would mention the headlines to her, reinforcing his understanding of her need to be included in his world and life.

As they ate their breakfast, Kitty was more talkative than usual and ate more slowly than Sam. She was remembering aloud pieces of the conversation about the addiction project that Sam had talked about the evening before. She was now not defensive about it, but feeling welcome as a participant, for after all, she was interested in everything that Sam did, and this was indeed a fascinating project. She knew she had let her neediness commandeer her emotions. However, the outcome had been positive, and this morning was tantamount to a fresh start.

Kitty had become intrigued about how monstrous addiction really is and how people become so easily hooked -- and like fish struggling on a hook, can't seem to break loose.

Together they played with a couple of dozen names for *the* monster, but could not become satisfied with any name as grippingly representative. It was Kitty who broke the code. "Sam," she exclaimed with an excitement of discovery, "we're missing the most cogent point. We're trying to make one size fit all. Don't you see? You've been talking about many addictions, so doesn't it make more sense to have many 'Hook Monsters'? A good artist could have a field day with an array of monsters."

"That's it! That's what they are, the Hook Monsters. You're great, that's genius. Thank you. I love you. This is fantastic. I'm going to love talking about the Hook Monsters. I can't wait to tell Doc. Oh, and thanks for breakfast, I really enjoyed it. And, especially thanks for last night. You were wonderful. Thanks for raising Peggy to be the wonderful daughter, mother to Brian, and wife to Al that she is. Thanks for marrying me and making my life what it is. I love you, Kitty."

"I love you too, Sam. And last night was indeed wonderful -- and thank you for our good life."

"Like you said, we're a team. I was thinking, Kitty, there's an ad in this morning's paper about the Bahamas. You've mentioned several times that you would like to vacation there. I should have listened before, but I'm going to try to listen better now. Being reminded how much you mean to me, I'm compelled to invite you to a vacation in the Bahamas for just the two of us. What do you say? Are you up for it? I bet we could really enjoy it."

"Why Sam, that's so sweet. Let's do it. The sooner, the better."

"Great. I can't wait. I better run. I don't want to be late for the tee time."

Breakfast dishes would languish in wait until Kitty's computer would oblige her with some preliminary information about the Bahamas. She read that there are seven hundred islands, world class beaches, beautiful resorts, numerous restaurants, scuba diving, snorkeling, swimming with dolphins, and even banking and business opportunities. Her interests leaned more to the former than the latter. She wanted a vacation, not another business trip. She hoped Sam would not get snared into a business arrangement there. She found considerable information on the islands and narrowed her interest to three islands: Abacos (Marsh Harbor), Grand Bahama (Freeport), and New Providence (Nassau). She decided to call her favorite travel agent, who told her that she had plenty of brochures that she could mail; or, if Kitty preferred, she could pick them up. Kitty was eager not to lose any momentum and decided to pick them up the following morning. Furthermore, Louise was always great with personal tips not to be found in the brochures. She would look forward to a visit with her.

Sam was playing golf with a noticeable refreshed and recharged spirit. David, one of the foursome, noticed and commented on Sam's mood and lower score. Sam simply said that he and Kitty were excitedly planning a trip to the Bahamas. To Sam's surprise, David had golf buddies and friends on Grand Bahama, where he visited frequently. He eagerly provided knowledge and shared suggestions. Sam soaked in the information and thought, *Kitty is sure to be surprised and* –he hoped – *pleased at what I have learned.*

Meanwhile, Kitty's mind was busily thinking of how to tell Sam what she had discovered. It was midafternoon, and she was rotely preparing her hot tea. Previously, she had concluded that this was an ingrained instinct left over from the "Old World." She never entertained a thought of giving it up, not even when Sam had teasingly observed that it was a continuous "old addiction."

Sam arrived home just in time to be offered a companion cup and gladly accepted. He had vowed to focus on anything that was mutual, sharing, supportive, encouraging, or praising to Kitty.

As they sat down, impatient eagerness prompted both of them to speak at once.

"Sam, I …"

"Kitty, I…"

Laughter enveloped them. "You first," Sam deferred to Kitty.

She thanked him for the offer and suggestion of a vacation in the Bahamas and emphasized how much it meant to her. She outlined for him all that she had learned and felt sure that one of three islands would suit their needs.

Sam expressed his delight in her happiness about their decision, but also his utter surprise that she had researched so much in such a short period of time. He confessed that he had hoped to impress her with his information while thinking she was still only in the dreaming stage. He was surprised with her initiative and did not miss the point that it underscored significant meaningfulness to her.

"Guess what?" Sam began, "The boys noticed how good I was feeling today. Also, that my game was improved. Thank you. I told them that I was up because we were planning a trip to the Bahamas. Wouldn't you know it? The small world concept kicked in. David has friends on Grand Bahama Island. He visits regularly and plays golf with them. He says it's a great place to visit. The Bahamians are friendly and hospitable. The dining is excellent, the prices are reasonable, there's plenty to do, and the golfing is great."

Kitty loved what she was hearing and that already they were narrowing their destination. And especially that he was not mentioning any business or banking opportunities.

"David stays at a friend's place. He gave me a web site that has pictures and a phone number. It's a small private place run by a lovely Welsh couple. It sounds ideal for us. Let's check it out."

Sam had been given a web site with pictures and information on the Bahamas.

www.mybahamavacation.com

CHAPTER 12

Addictions and Monsters

SAM EAGERLY ANTICIPATED the next weekly meeting with Dr. Lavoy and without even chitchat, excitedly began talking about the monsters.

"Doc, Kitty has conceptualized our plan and visualizes the monster concept in a clever manner. She figures monsters are marketable -- and did you notice I said plural? She thinks we can do a different monster for each addiction. The more we talked about it, the more I liked her idea."

"Great, Sam! Tell me more."

Sam outlined the entire concept, pointing out that he thought the applications were endless.

"Good idea!" Lavoy continued. "I know some artists we can contact to see if they can give us some ideas about monster concepts. We could use them for posters, or maybe even on the book cover. We might even sell monster sculptures. People could use them as gifts or as reminders."

"That will thrill Kitty. What's the next step, Doc?"

Lavoy said, "First, we need to finish our outline. We can work on the monsters later." Doc reviewed where they were with listing the addictions and creating brief outlines. They decided to add some introductory remarks for other addictions, and add to their list.

"Gambling is a particularly troubling addiction. About one-half of one percent of the US population is addicted to gambling, or roughly one and a half million people. These people are so out of control that they usually squander all their possessions and lose their families. Another five to ten million gamble unrealistically and should be considered to have a gambling problem.

"It is estimated that promiscuous and unrestrained sex claims fifteen million US adults as addicts. The gender ratio is two to one, male to female. This one is more difficult to see, diagnose, understand, or treat.

"Shopping addiction afflicts as many as ten to fifteen million US adults. Men are tempted to laugh or nod knowingly, but the facts indicate it's about a one to one ratio. Infomercials and Madison Avenue are collaborative enablers.

"Does anyone doubt the addictive powers of food? Have you ever fought with your own willpower and lost to the satiation provided by that chocolate bar, piece of cake, or some other scrumptious dessert? I think we all have. What usually follows is the nagging guilt and, not infrequently, weight gain. Many evolve to being overweight or obese. The national percentage of overweight people now has risen to sixty-four and one-half percent with an average of about half of them -- or thirty and one-half percent of the population -- being obese. Obesity has now become a problem for many of our children. Some suggest that the snack food industry is aware of and takes advantage of the addictive attributes of some snack food ingredients.

"Pornography is a growing, spreading addiction. The Internet broadened the access and accelerated the growth. We now estimate approximately ten percent of the population is addicted to pornography. Like sex addiction, it is often difficult to spot and treat. Often when spouses are suspicious or even catch their partner viewing pornography, they are reluctant to force treatment because of embarrassment.

"Internet addiction was first mentioned in jest. Now, however, we realize that it is a serious addiction problem, often with disastrous consequences. Many people lose their jobs, friends, relationships, and even marriages. We see similar addictive behavior in the lower animals. Monkeys and mice push and pull levers in increasingly difficult patterns to attain greater rewards.

"Running is addictive for some. It is thought that a high results from the release of internal endorphins, the pleasure hook that is responsible for this addiction.

"Also, racing is another sport in which the 'thrill' causes an outpouring of endorphins and adrenaline. There has to be an addictive element at play when one reaches the point of knowing that the risk of accidental death is high and the racer continues the pursuit of joyous rewards, essentially ignoring the obvious danger.

"And Sam, I must add one more addiction that will be new for us to discuss as it is not an official diagnosis. That addiction is 'shoes.' This was first publicly noted by Imelda's famous shoe collection. Now, however, we know that many people have hordes of shoes. Just the other day, my wife and I were having a meal at a pancake house and the waitress began obsessively, incessantly talking about shoes and her 'problem' with shoes. She told us that when her boyfriend saw her closet full of shoes and shoes stacked in corners, he bolted and never came back. She also kept on talking about the best places to shop for shoes, not just local markets, but on the Internet as well. It seems to me that this is a real ongoing addiction."

"So there really are many addictions," Sam agreed. I suppose every addiction is a monster to someone."

"That makes sense, Sam. Let's come back to this next time. By the way, how is Brian?"

"Oh, he's great. I have a date with him to play miniature golf this afternoon. He plays golf so often; he must be hoping to be a doctor, huh? You're a psychiatrist....Am I supposed to let him win?"

"At least once in a while," Lavoy offered.

"Thanks for the advice."

CHAPTER **13**

Kitty Joins the War

KITTY WAS PLEASED that Sam and Doc liked the multiple monster concept. Her involvement and inquisitiveness pressed her to ask if Sam and the doctor had begun to name any of the monsters.

"No, not yet. Have you got some ideas?"

Indeed Kitty did have some thoughts. "Each monster should have a name and all names should follow a pattern. They should be simple, easy to remember, sketchable, produceable, and symbolic as gifts. We must, however, have a way to subdue their power. Since we can't get rid of our monsters, we must find a way to neutralize their power and danger. Addictions never die; they just have to be controlled for life so that they are impotent."

"I like your ideas," Sam complimented Kitty.

"I've been listening to you and reading as well. Sam, I've thought about the years we've had to deal with your cigarette addiction. I'm convinced you never appreciated the imposition that your addiction was on me or Peggy, especially since we weren't smokers. I'm not fussing at you or trying to put you on a guilt trip. What I am saying is that your treatment approach should include the family.

"Think about treatment programs, Sam. Most have testimonials that are just someone's story. A recovering addict confesses his addiction and outlines his or her path to destruction and ruin. It could have been family problems, financial, professional, spiritual, physical, or mental health problems. Then he goes on to tell of his recovery path and perhaps how difficult it is to reintegrate to substance-free living. Then hope and encouragement are offered to the afflicted followed by admonitions to those not yet afflicted, but vulnerable."

"That about sums it up, Kitty."

"It shouldn't stop there. You know, AA has Al-Anon. Your approach should be more inclusive upfront. I'm not applying for a job, but if you could construct your speeches so that the spouse or child of a recovering person could be part of the talk, wouldn't that be better? In our case, for example, I could talk of my disgust for tobacco clothes and breath. Perhaps drop some humor about some promising moments that got killed. I could wonder aloud how many contracts or work situations might have been unknowingly spoiled. I could talk of my anger and resentment at you for voluntarily bringing on your illness. I could talk lovingly of your entering recovery and my learning how to support recovery, like we're doing it together, and learning how to be aware of myself when enabling you and my need to recover from my enabling habits. I don't say it's all right anymore, I don't offer to pick up a carton of cigarettes while I'm out shopping, I don't clean ashtrays, and I don't make excuses for you or your cough. I would make an impassioned plea for the spouses, children, friends, or significant others to be a concerned partner pushing for prevention or recovery, as the case might be."

"Oh Kitty, I'm such a fool. How utterly blind I was. Even when I knew it bothered you, I rationalized that you understood, and you were used to it and that it didn't matter to you. I am so sorry, please forgive me."

"Like I said, we both have plenty of faults in your addiction. The main thing now is that we both are invested in what amounts to *our* recovery. Too many people still see it as one-sided. I know it's not just your recovery, but ours. If it is this bad for smoking, it likely is even worse for those families dealing with narcotics and alcohol."

"You need to start coming to the meetings with me and the Doc."

"No, no. But if you think it has merit, we can continue to pursue a joint presentation. Oh, that reminds me. When you do your talk, if you do a monograph, it might be a good idea to have visuals of the individual monsters as you mention each addiction."

"I like that."

"I've been thinking of some names, see what you think. Smoky, Coffey, Alkie, Druggie, Gambly, Sexly, Shoppy, Foody, Pornly, Netly, Runly, Racely, Shoely."

"Not bad. I like them."

"I do think the artists will have to be clever. They are monsters, but are also supposed to be appealing and seductive. Each monster must have a hook. The left hand should have the hook, but it shouldn't be quickly obvious. Also, it has to be constructed so that it won't be dangerous to small children if they play with them."

"Kitty, thanks for being on my team."

"I wouldn't miss it."

"Oh, Thomas called. He says he needs our help. He wants you to call him. Let's be careful. Don't co-sign anything with him."

"Copy that and ten-four, my dear. I'll call him on the way to my visit with Doc."

"I hope your plans go well. 'Bye, I love you."

"You too."

CHAPTER **14**

Family Snares

SAM DECIDED HE could multitask and save time. He prided himself on organization skills. En route to Dr. Lavoy's he phoned his nephew, Thomas. To his knowledge, Thomas had been seriously depressed at least three times. He also remembered his being in rehab for drug and alcohol treatment. He became manic once in '93. That happened when he got on cocaine and became involved with a pole dancer. When his wife started asking questions, he ran away to Texas with the dancer. He maxed out his credit cards and eventually sank into an abysmal depression. His girlfriend found him unresponsive with an empty bottle of Sominex. She called 911; the rescue team came and transported him to the hospital. That close call had been instrumental in turning his life around. After a stint in rehab he remained clean for a few months, but then started to drink again. He was arrested for DUI. The policeman even told him to get help. His company's Employee Assistance Program sent him to a counselor. Hopefully, this call didn't mean that he had relapsed and was in trouble.

Sam drew a couple of deep breaths during the three rings before Thomas answered.

"Hello?"

"Hello Thomas, this is Uncle Sam. I'm returning your call. It's good to hear from you," Sam forced the words out, yet he was able to sound genuine.

69 ➤

"It's good to talk to you -- how is Aunt Kitty?"

"Oh fine, fine; still putting up with me. She's a strong woman."

"That she is. Are you okay, Uncle Sam?"

"I am. In fact, I've probably never felt better, maybe since I was sixteen. How's your family? You've got some teenagers now, don't you?"

"I do, they're basically okay. Karen's a freshman at Jefferson State this year. She's great. Benjamin, though, is having some problems. That's what I'm calling about, Uncle Sam. You and Aunt Kitty seem to have it together. Peggy's great. Y'all raised her right. Ben -- well, he's seventeen and going on thirty, but acting like a fourteen-year-old. He's been smoking and we caught him drinking. He's irritable; he sasses his mama and me. He's probably smoking marijuana, and we know he is experimenting with harder drugs. He stays in his room and listens to awful-sounding music. Yesterday he was expelled from school for the remainder of the year. We try to talk to him, but he says we have no right . . . it's his life and he's not doing anything different than we did. And all his friends agree they're just having some fun."

Sam was already anticipating what was coming. Referring to Peggy was the tip off.

"Anyway, being here with us just seems to be making bad matters worse. Lauren and I talked it over and we were wondering if Ben might benefit from staying with you and Aunt Kitty for a few weeks. He has always admired you. We don't know where else to turn. We would be awfully grateful. It might be just what he needs. We would be glad to help with room and board. It's just, well, I guess he just needs to see what normal is. It wouldn't have to be long. What do you think?"

"You flatter me and Kitty, Thomas. I'm real sorry Ben's giving you and Lauren such a problem. Have you been to counseling, and have you thought of a rehab program for him?"

"We have been in counseling. He has resisted, of course; thinks it's a joke. He sabotages treatment. He's just not ready yet. We thought a different approach might work better. Would you consider it? I'm afraid he might wind up in juvenile detention if we don't do something."

"Thomas, that's a tall order. Let me talk it over with Kitty. We have no training nor experience in doing this sort of thing. Anything could happen and, you know, we would be feeling responsible and terrible if something bad did happen."

"I know, Uncle Sam. That's the way we feel. We just need help. We won't hold you responsible. We'll be grateful that you tried."

"Well, okay. Let us think on it. Kitty and I will consult on it and pray about it and get back to you." Sam couldn't wait to get to Lavoy's office to discuss this before he mentioned it to Kitty.

Lavoy listened without interruption until Sam had literally relayed word for word all Thomas had said, in addition to his own dreadful thoughts.

"Sam," Lavoy began, "I can't comfort you in this. You're in a no-win situation. Trouble begets trouble. The seeds for all of this were already fertile back during the days that Thomas was in college when Eileen tried to intervene and rescue Thomas. He may not be remembering how he rebuffed her offer to help at that time. Now his own son is refusing him. If you don't help, you're a louse, of course. And what is family for? The guilt feelings will encompass you and maybe even be thrown at you. If you do accommodate their needs and wishes, you are inviting grief and turmoil into your home. You will be adding another stress on top of what you and Kitty have barely managed to survive. If Kitty doesn't put her foot down and you give in, please put down firm rules; loving, but firm, and guarantee yourself, Kitty, Thomas, and Ben that you will enforce them. You will not let them be bent or broken. And know this, Sam: he will figure a way to test you. It will be just below your threshold of tolerance. He will see if he can get you to bend just a little. If you do, the game of escalation will have begun. That would be a terrible thing for you, Sam. If you are firm, he will likely test you again and then again. These kids -- let me say these addicts -- are clever. They are masters in sizing people up and figuring out just how far people can be pushed. Don't fall for it, Sam."

"I'm listening, Doc."

"Remember this: any subterfuge you might have used hiding your smoking a cigarette was kindergarten compared to the tricks and con tactics these devious druggies use."

"Okay, I'm forewarned."

"It's up to you to be forearmed."

"I understand."

"Let me tell you about four teenagers I treated in the seventies. All were rebellious and using drugs. I counseled all the parents with the same advice and admonition that I just told you. Two sets of the parents listened and followed my advice by anticipating the challenge, but they did not give in. Those two teenagers turned out okay.

"The other two sets of parents felt that was too rigid and, after all, felt they were only bending the rules slightly, so they gave in. Both teens escalated their behavioral problems and eventually were in legal difficulty. One, in fact, was such a con artist that the judge even felt sympathy for him. When he stood before that judge for the third time, the judge told him that he had no choice except to sentence him to prison time. The judge actually cried as he pronounced the sentence."

"Is that what you mean about them being con artists, Doc?"

"It is -- sometimes they fool the experts. Most of us have to admit to being hoodwinked. Sam," Lavoy continued, "I'll be giving a talk on addiction to a group of mixed professionals on Thursday evening. The group is composed of therapists and counselors, some of whom are recovering from some form of addiction. Why don't you join me? It might help you understand drug addiction."

If anything, the discussion and preparation banter had the unintended effect of feeding into Sam's confident attitude. He felt he could do anything that he put his mind to. By the time he had reached home and was relaying the situation to Kitty, he had convinced himself that he and Kitty would handle anything that Ben might do or try with them. He rationalized, *If I refuse to do this isn't that refusing to do the walk after giving the talk? After all, the Doc and I are commit-*

ted to fighting addiction.

Kitty listened quietly. In fact, so reserved was she that Sam finally heard her silence. Neither was she applauding. It was Sam's nephew. She would not want to appear unwilling to help Sam's family, especially since he was obviously inclined to agree to bring Ben into their home. She wondered, *Has Sam considered the negative impact on us, or the potential problems?*

"I have prattled on too long and you've been good to patiently listen, but I do want your input. I told Thomas the answer had to be our joint decision and that it was a tall order requiring careful and prayerful deliberation."

"Thank you for not making me the potential bad guy."

"I wouldn't put you in that kind of situation."

"I didn't want to interrupt. You sounded almost enthused, but I admit the prospect sounds scary. I must have a hundred what-ifs."

"Frankly, me too. First, you and I meet with Thomas, Lauren, and Ben. We spell it out. We want to help, but it's our house and our home. We've made it the way we like it, the way it works for us. We can share it, but we can't and won't change it for Ben or Thomas. Second, we share. We help Ben, but Ben helps us. Everybody has responsibilities. That includes Ben if he's living here. We abide by the house rules, do our chores, and we don't grumble."

Sam convinced Kitty that he would be stern and not let Thomas and Ben take undue advantage of them.

The meeting was arranged for Sunday afternoon and true to his word, Sam spoke the same words to Ben and Thomas that he had promised her. The meeting was planned after some preliminary discussion with Thomas. He and Lauren would bring Ben to their house, where they would have a full discussion of the possibility of Ben living with them and what the rules would be should everyone decide to go through with this plan.

CHAPTER 15

Our Addicted Brain

SAM WAS COMFORTED that he would hear Dr. Lavoy's talk prior to meeting with Ben and his parents. Sam had discussed the dangers of smoking mostly with friends and acquaintances. He was not yet giving talks in the traditional stand up and speak mode. He wondered how different it would be. He tried to guess how Dr. Lavoy would approach drug addicts: those who use heroin, cocaine, crack cocaine, Dilaudid, OxyContin, Lortab, etc. Would he have credibility, being *only* an ex-smoker? Lavoy was introduced and approached the podium. Sam listened intently.

"Fellow addicts, ladies and gentlemen, we have something in common. We are at war with an addiction monster residing within us. We must learn all we can from each other. I have something to teach you. Listen up. Addiction comes to us in many forms and through various avenues. Furthermore, its consequences are varied and seemingly tailored to each individual with timing, intensity, and ultimate end result. So while each of us as addicts has the same common core -- namely addiction -- we are, nevertheless, each and every one different in our addiction. Each of us is different even from those addicted to the very same substance. You are individually as different from the person sitting next to you as you are from me. Yet my addiction was -- excuse me, **is** -- nicotine.

"We are not such simple creatures that all we need is a steady, timely, ample supply of our DOC (drug of choice). We want our fix, whether it is twenty cigarettes per day or six 80 mg OxyContin, or whatever. Oh no, we are masters of confounding nuances, which relate to and act on our individual needs, such as pain, social anxiety, irritability, tension, mood, energy, perception, sleep, interest or lack thereof, etc. We say we are uncomfortable without THE substance, whether heroin, alcohol, tobacco, benzodiazepines, etc. That's why addictionologists talk of having a 'comfortable sobriety.' If your drug of choice is part of your coping mechanism, then without your substance you will be as uncomfortable as a person who has lost his artificial leg."

Danny, a meeting attendee, raised his hand, simultaneously speaking. "It's not just uncomfortable. Man, I don't even feel like myself when I'm clean. When I use I feel more normal, more in control, more likeable. And it's not like I'm feeling high. I'm harder to get along with when I'm clean. My kids say I'm fussy."

"That's a good segue to another point that many addicts never hear, or at least, never learn. So hear me, fellow addicts. It will surprise some of you to know that the fact is, we addicts are **not** normal when we are clean. Did you hear me? We are not normal when we are clean. It is imperative that you know this and deal with it if you expect to ever be able to live a secure and comfortable clean life. This is vastly different from what your family and some counselors and doctors will tell you. But stay with me, I tell you the truth. Please note, the *cure* is from the feeling of being abnormal in the clean state. This freedom is attainable and sustainable. I'll explain it to you in detail because if you don't know and understand this concept, your chances of relapse are at least two out of three. Look to your right and then to your left. Which of the three of you could make it just doing what you've done before? But I tell you, if you learn today's information and are motivated and follow a methodological treatment plan such as NA, AA or a rehabilitation program, then you may look right, left, front, and back and know that four of the five of you will likely become comfortably clean for life. Now how many of you are interested? These odds are much better, don't you think?

"Let's start with the aforementioned amputee. We will call him Joe. Maybe he's GI Joe. He is 29 years old. At age 23, he caught a .50-caliber machine gun bullet at the top of his right knee. What remained of the knee and everything below it could not be salvaged. An above-knee amputation was required. The initial loss was uncomfortable and painful, physically and psychologically. In rehab, he learned new coping skills and was fitted with a prosthetic leg. Eventually, he learned to walk and even to run. In fact, so normally that strangers would not be aware of his having a prosthetic leg unless they saw it. Oh, were you listening? Did you hear me use the word 'normally'? Yes, to others, and even to Joe, he had become 'normal' as a person with an artificial leg. He was not fully, biologically whole and normal in the original sense, but biophysiologically and biometrically, he was functionally 'normal.' Something had been added to his body which he had now used for an extended period of time, long enough for full assimilation into routine expectation, use, and habit. The new part, the foreign substance, was accepted, anticipated, and used regularly. It was now part of him. If it was temporarily out of reach or out of working order, it was sorely missed. You see where I'm going with this, don't you? If it were to be confiscated or rendered impossible to keep for any reason, Joe would – guess what? Feel how?– abnormal, of course, in much the same way as when he lost his biological leg.

"When our life and routine are substantially interrupted, such as Joe's prosthetic leg being taken away or my cigarettes being henceforth forbidden or your opiates forsaken in favor of health or family, etc., then we have lost or given up a significant part of ourselves. Any added part which we have adapted and, over time, assimilated into ourselves actually becomes a reformed or adapted normalcy inclusive of our new part and its regular usage. So, indeed, we addicts **are** correct to say that we 'feel not ourselves, that is abnormal,' when we are clean. Without that part of us, the prosthesis, cigarette, opiate, alcohol, benzodiazepine, etc., we are not our current usual or adapted *normal* self. We are abnormal. It's not weird at all when you understand the logic behind it.

"The foregoing is extremely important for you to understand. For one thing, you have known it all along at the feeling level, but non-addicts and even some counselors will debate you, which means argue with you, which means lecture you, that your normal state is the clean state. To help them and us understand this relative normalcy, we need to look more discerningly at what is our normal state.

"Is normal the same for any of us? Look at the different stages of life: infant, child, teenager, young adult, adult, middle-life, senior, and geriatric. Isn't normal different in each stage? Of course it is. Besides that, our normalcy is based on various other circumstances – climate, education, experience, family, genetics, upbringing, etc. Looking at all of this, we clearly see the relativity of normalcy, and hence, the normal vs. abnormal state of feeling with and without our addictive substance. Once our bodies have adapted to our substance of choice, our normalcy includes the substance, just as Joe adapted to his prosthetic leg. Another appropriate example could be the person with an intact body using steroids to change the body strength and thereby becoming different and requiring a different or new feeling of normalcy. So please grasp the concept that normalcy for us is a dynamic state of flux, of which addiction is one of the powerful factors. However, you must know, believe, and work the premise that indeed addiction **is** controllable.

"To more fully comprehend this, you need to have an understanding of time as it relates to the reshaping of what our personal perception of normal is. So let's return to Joe for more insight. After Joe's amputation, he was astounded because he continued to have a sense of having a complete leg. Consciously, he knew the leg was missing and visually he could see that it was absent. Yet, in his 'mind's eye,' he could still see the leg. He learned from his doctors that this was called 'phantom limb.' And, in fact, he was lucky because some amputees also have phantom pain in the lost limb as if it were still there. Joe was also taught that over time the phantom would shrink and finally disappear. For Joe, that took about two years. Joe described the process as an uncanny phenomenon. It was, he said, like the leg slowly disappearing. Everything became smaller and shorter over time until it completely diminished and reabsorbed into the stump. At the end, it seemed as if his foot and, lastly, his toes disappeared back into his stump.

"Again, his doctors explained that even though the leg was gone, the brain continued to have the full complement of brain assigned to that lost part of the leg. Since the brain remained active, the leg continued to be visible in the mind's eye. The brain, over time, learns that its function has been rendered useless and so it gradually shuts down. The disappearance time frame is proportional to the amount of brain assigned to a part. Let's say, for example, there are 100 times more neurons assigned to the foot and toes than there are to the upper part of the missing leg. Because the smaller set of the neurons lose all function quicker than the larger set, it would appear to the mind's eye exactly as Joe described it, i.e. the foot and the toes would be the last to disappear.

"This is the scientific explanation of what you have been feeling. It is of the utmost importance that you understand it. We actually use functional MRIs (magnetic resonance imaging) to see the brain's function change over time and to a large extent rewire itself, even putting those unused neurons to new uses. So when you give up your narcotic and I my tobacco and Ben his alcohol and Helen her benzodiazepine tranquilizer, it doesn't just suddenly exit the brain or the mind's eye. It will take time. Different substances produce different intensities of addiction, for example, benzodiazepines vs. heroin.

"Likewise, different people have varying susceptibility to substances rooted in their genetics, their nurturing, and their individual psychological makeup. To illustrate, let's look at two individual addicts. Individual A is addicted to cocaine. Individual B is addicted to marijuana. Individual A, with his first snort, felt a euphoric high that he had never even imagined possible. He was generally an unmotivated, uninspired person. He immediately wanted another snort. He became a frequent user and even a dealer. He used until all of his money, friends, and family were used up.

"Individual B started to smoke some weed in college. At first, it was no big deal, just a social thing. After about six months, he noticed that he wanted a joint more often and particularly when feeling stressed. There was no genetic predisposition. He was generally psychologically sound; but initially, just being with the boys, he began to use. The increased use was insidious and subconscious. Eventually its use became expected and standard, but then a craving developed.

"Individual A would be expected to have a tremendous brain involvement with cocaine. Therefore, the deprogramming or deactivation will likely be over an extended period of time. Individual A is likely to be tense, irritable, uncomfortable, and very prone to relapse. Individual B, on the other hand, is likely to have less brain involvement and, therefore, a quicker adaptation with a better chance of staying clean.

"As an addict, you, I, our families, the insurance companies, government programs, etc., all want to know how long it takes to cure addiction. Well, one thing we have learned. **There is no cure.** Once addicted, always addicted. Addiction is for life.

"What we can cure is the perception of normalcy. We must realize that our normalcy feeling is warped by the addiction and is unhealthy for us. It is necessary to reestablish a goal of normalcy without the substance. Then we must design a treatment course that returns us to the state of being that promotes living a comfortable, sober, clean life. How long it takes to reach that level of comfort is definitely an individual measure. However, there is a rule of thumb that we can use. It is instructive to be aware of this, as it gives hope and courage to your patience. Roughly, for each year or a little less, the intensity of comfortableness increases by about fifty percent. That means the brain's effort to support the addiction reduces about fifty percent per year. This means the **comfort level** is zero on the quit day, 50 percent after 12 months, 75 percent after 24 months, 87.5

percent after 36 months, 93.75 percent after 48 months, and 96.6 percent after 60 months. You see from this, it never reaches 100 percent. But you can also surmise that an optimistic goal would be that between two to three years one begins to become confident of one's ability to stay clean. This also clearly demonstrates why those first two to three years are painfully difficult.

"In the same manner, the cure from addiction never reaches zero. As long as the body has any memory or fragment of addiction left, it is forever ready to spring back into full force. So if and when the body encounters the substance again, it fully rebounds in the same way that an allergy, unchallenged for decades, can react strongly enough to cause anaphylactic shock and death. So all the brain circuitry would be instantly reactivated and the desire would return to 100 percent -- some say even with a vengeance.

"Your brain never quits working for you, even when it is unknowingly plotting against you. My addiction illustrates this. I quit smoking in '72, but in 1984, while sick with mono, I awoke one night dreaming that I was smoking. I realized that this had been a recurring dream during my illness. The take-home message on this is that when we are weakened in any manner, whether physically or psychologically, our intelligent brain will try to take advantage of our weakest moment and return us to our substance of choice. You see, your brain is attempting to 'fix' you and stimulate your pleasure center while subconsciously rationalizing that you are really sick, you feel bad, and you need a lift out of your unhappy state. Besides -- it's just for right now when you need it so badly; no one will know and you won't make it a habit. Your brain is ignoring the sure total recall, the powerful rebound, and the damage that ensues by reactivating the entire addictive process. It craves instant gratification.

"At this point, your conscious brain **does** know better and **must** take control and take charge. Call your sponsor, call anybody -- your minister, your friend -- but don't succumb to the temptation. Unfortunately, your intelligence, knowledge, and consciousness have no mechanism to call into play your emotional reinforcement.

That's where a buddy comes in. Social contact engages the emotion, which is a real plus in the AA twelve-step program. A big danger here for most addicts is their old user friends. This is the moment they wait for. They know all the slick lines to ease the hook back into your addiction.

"The brain is a phenomenally capable organ. In overall ability, it remains the most enviable object in the universe. Computers are faster in calculation -- now more than a quadrillion per second -- but the brain is vastly superior in all the nuances and intangible associations. It is our servant and works tirelessly for us. Just for our purposes here, focus on its efforts to increasingly satisfy the needs of the pleasure center. You have heard 'whatever makes you happy.' This could be the mantra of the brain. Other considerations do compete and can be explored in another setting, including spiritual, cultural, loyalty, honor, species preservation, etc. The brain has one huge disadvantage that a computer would not. The brain, perhaps programmed hedonistically by some personalities but not by others, will use its awesome power and resources to continue reproducing intense pleasure or reducing displeasure or pain, favoring immediate gratification and seeming to ignore or disregard known long-term dangers and detriments. A computer would disconnect or 'tilt' when in such a quandary between immediate intense gratification versus postponed, though vastly enhanced, rewards. If we could only implant a 'tilt' chip, we would really be on to something.

"Spirituality is likely the closest thing humans have to a tilt chip. One who is properly grounded in spirituality has more power to call on for help. Their emotion is engaged and enhanced by this unseen, but strongly felt presence, especially in one's conscience.

"The advantage of the brain is its ability to learn by education, observation, and experience; and thereby, to mature, and postpone gratification in order to achieve better results and benefits, hence an eventual superior gratification. This process is arrested by addiction. Recovery reengages the maturing process. Working recovery is a day by day painful and tedious process of returning to a clean, more natural normalcy.

"When we discontinue our addictive substance of choice, not only does the pleasure cease, but in its place comes discomfort and displeasure, often quite severe and at times even dangerous, causing seizures or death. Before modern medicine, four out of ten people died in delirium tremens from alcohol withdrawal. On your quit day, keep this in mind. Remember that your comfortable sobriety level will be 0. Your addiction level will be 100 percent. Your goal is to reverse the order.

"With what you have learned from this talk, you can knowledgeably make a rational decision to beat addiction.

"You must make your own decision.

"You must plan and plot your recovery path.

"Recovery must include comfortable, sober, clean living.

"Your timeline must be reasonable.

"You should use a recognized treatment program such as AA.

"You should find spiritual contentment.

"You must include a guide or sponsor.

"You must not look back.

"You must not relapse. At the least it means starting over, at the worst it means death.

"Your goal has to be not just being substance-free, but sobriety plus, in which the plus is up to you. Is it rediscovering your natural normalcy, i.e. recovering yourself? Is it better health? Salvaging family? Longer life? Improved spiritual qualities? To repair relationships? Maybe a dedication to righting past wrongs, or perhaps a personal crusade against addiction? All of which, may I assure you, can be genuinely satisfying and rewarding.

"Your life cannot be fully enjoyed or appreciated while you are in the grip of addiction, not by yourself, family, colleagues, or society. I call on you to embrace recovery and a helpful buddy. Join the war on addiction: yours, mine, and ours. I will be available for personal questions or discussion. Good luck to each of you."

Sam could not have anticipated the content of the speech. He now understood his addiction and its power over him much better than he had before.

A line formed immediately to have personal time with Dr. Lavoy. Sam positioned himself so as to overhear and absorb as much information as possible.

CHAPTER 16

Moving In

THOMAS AND LAUREN brought Ben to Sam and Kitty's home. This was moving in day. The inauspicious occasion had understandably provoked anxiety in Kitty and Sam, but not one of the four of them had even an inkling of how naïve they were about the strain and stress that were stalking them. The many vicissitudes of drug addiction and family dysfunction had flourished for years, but now had culminated in a frightening crisis. Wrong excels easily when right passively does nothing. Right triumphs over wrong only by a great and sustained effort. With drug addiction, the amount of effort required is universally underestimated. "Just quit smoking. Just don't drink anymore. Just say no." Simple, right? Don't we wish? Generally, there will be several failed attempts before the family or the addict gives in to defeat and turns to professionals. Many families and friends tend to think there is nothing they can do. If they just "stand back" and give the user time, it will somehow run its course and disappear as if it were an inconvenient phase. They are consciously oblivious to the kindling factor: the longer the addiction (or nearly any illness) is unchecked, the more it grows, and consequently, the less likely it is that there will be a satisfactory outcome.

Tension was palpable as Thomas, Lauren, and Ben arrived, bringing in two suitcases. Sam and Kitty had asked for a joint rules session so there could be no mistake about what the goals and rules would be. They detailed what would be allowed and what would not be allowed. Even Thomas was uneasy about how strict Sam and Kitty might be with Ben.

Thomas thanked Kitty and Sam. He then self-revealed his difficult fight to overcome his multiple addictions. "I was what is known as a poly-substance abuser. I did drugs, alcohol, tobacco -- whatever made me feel good." He recounted how difficult his life had been compared to what it could have been, including the family lifestyle that so permissively and stupidly had allowed Ben to grow up thinking that they were normal. "Yet now we realize that Lauren and I both were simply making excuses and enabling Ben just as I had been enabled."

Thomas pointed out the difference in the accomplishments in life and status, for example, between Sam and Kitty and himself and Lauren. He noted that it was due strictly to his immediate and ever-present focus on one of his cravings. Alcohol, drugs, or cigarettes -- each in some way interfered with family, jobs, school, relationships, and even his spiritual health. He was only at this late date beginning to realize the need to rekindle a satisfaction in all of these needs. He thought it important to reassure Sam and Kitty in part by continuing his firm commitment to recovery. He knew that it was also important for Ben that he continue his clean and sober life. Now with two years behind him, his own confidence was building.

Poignantly and emotionally, he then said he was handling himself with the help of AA and others, but he was lost with helping Ben and it was tearing his heart out to watch his son screw up his life in the very same way that he himself had done years earlier. Thomas noted that, like most addicts' parents, he was blind for too long with denial about Ben's addictions, symptoms, and their escalation. He saw this as his last best hope for Ben before it was too late and he wound up in prison or long-term rehab -- or worse, possibly even dead. He and Lauren were immensely grateful to Sam and Kitty for helping in their family crisis.

"Thank you for all of that, Thomas." Sam had not expected that prelude to the substantive conversation he was planning to have with them. He had definitely given thought as to what he was going to say to Ben. Conversation should always be fluid, and flow based on what has gone before. Therefore, this would take a little different tack than Sam had intended. Life and its events follow a stepwise progression, and so should we in our thinking and discussions.

Sam began, "You mentioned the constant array of problems that relate to drug and alcohol abuse. That is an important point. We must not forget the less immediate consequences: interference in schools, family, friends, finances, and roadblocks to future possibilities.

"Some problems require long periods of time before the damage is visible. Examples include my lung cancer from smoking, or cirrhosis and dementia from drinking, and hepatitis from drugs. In our youth, we feel, think, and act in the minute – the here and now. The future is somehow sequestered safely away so that we will arrive there only at some later, more opportune time. It is the meanest trick our mind plays on our youth, invoking the full comfort of denial as we collude with danger.

"So, Ben, if you are listening, you know by now that your mom and dad and Kitty and I probably know you better than you thought, and likely better than you know yourself. We know who you are – an addict. We know where you are – with one foot in hedonism and the other in denial. We know where you have been. Like your dad said, he is sorry for his shortcomings with you, but even so he had no control over the choices you made with your own free will – drugs, alcohol, cigarettes and, probably, girls -- despite his and your mom's warning. You, as we, live in a permissive, complacent society and a dysfunctional family. That along with your arrogant attitude, 'I'll do as I please,' has brought you to this here and now time, place, and situation."

Sam continued, "Okay, tell me straight, why now? I want to hear from each of you. Why is this the do or die moment? Have you hit bottom, Ben?"

Ben quickly tried to make a plausible statement. "No, it's nothing like that. Dad's just afraid that Mom will divorce him. She's always after him to make me quit drinking. He knows I've turned over a new leaf and I'm going to be a responsible person from now on. Mom doesn't believe me and says if he lets me drink again, she's going to leave him. I really understand that things are bad and I'm going to be better, Mom."

Thomas, following Ben's lead, spoke before Lauren. "There's more to it than that, Ben. We have sent you to private counseling, the school has counseled you, and we've sent you to an outpatient rehabilitation program. You haven't listened and you haven't changed. I've tried to be understanding, but I've been too lenient. When our friend, Marty Keely, the policeman, rang our doorbell the other night, that was my lowest point. My heart skipped a few beats. I didn't know if he was coming to take you away or arrest me for child neglect. You didn't know it, but Marty originally arrested me. He sent me to Dr. Lita Clark, and because of them I got started in recovery and I'm doing fine.

"He stopped by to tell me what he had done. They arrested your three friends. Vaughn, only nineteen, is facing felony charges for possession. Felons lose their right to vote, Ben. Most good jobs are unavailable to them. Wolford, only eighteen, was in the car and arrested and he's also going to be in trouble. David Noble is seventeen, like you. A minister's son; how does that happen? He will go to juvenile court. He will likely be sent for treatment. Vaughn and Wolford snitched on you. Yeah, they told him that you'd been in the car and they'd just let you out before they were arrested. Marty decided to come get you after dark and without the flashing lights and to take you to jail, which he did. He wanted to show you where you could wind up and he told you about the legal problems that you just missed. He also told you that you were sure to be facing those charges or more or worse if you didn't get help. He locked you inside the jail cell for an hour. He did you and us a favor. Your mother had a right to put her foot down on both of us. That's why we're here now."

Sam took that opening to expand the dangers. "That was a one in a thousand favor, Ben. That alone should wake you up. If those boys stay on their current path they will wind up in prison or dead. You, Ben, are traveling that same path with them. You call them friends. I call them criminals and addicts. The Nobles are scared to death. We know the Nobles, Ben."

Now it was Lauren's turn. "I don't know if Ben hit bottom, but I sure did. When you see a policeman take your son away in a police car, there aren't enough tears or words to tell you how broken my heart was. I forgot about the way you pitted me against your dad, constantly triangulating us so that we were either mad at each other or resenting each other. At that moment, I just loved you and felt hurt for you and wanted to protect you. We're lucky he brought you back. The other three are facing such problems that I don't know if your dad and I could have handled them, let alone you. I realized after he brought you back and we relaxed and had time to realize that what your dad had been trying to do was to love you into quitting while I was trying to parent you into changing. You saw that as nagging and not understanding, rather than our love and concern. I wanted your dad to send you to one of those wilderness treatment centers for six months or a year. I hear they work pretty well. Your dad came up with this idea. I was reluctant and still am for a variety of reasons, not the least of which is the imposition on Aunt Kitty and Uncle Sam. Thomas talked me into giving it a try and that's why we're here."

Sam had gotten more than he expected. "We won't look at it as an imposition, Lauren. We're family. Ben, that was an awfully close call with the law, and you're only seventeen years old. You know and we know that you have two paths in front of you and you have to choose. We will do all we can to guide you to the best choice, but ultimately, it is your choice. We can guide, but we can't force.

"It is difficult to change. It requires effort, desire, determination, and a focused goal. It causes anxiety and pain. A simple example would be when you learned to ride a bicycle. While you were comfortable walking, you were envious of the fun others were having riding their bikes. At first, the thought of trying to ride a bicycle makes

one anxious and doubtful. The process took effort, work, and provoked laughter from family and friends. It also likely brought the pain
of more than one embarrassing mishap. But the effort paid off; you
rode the bicycle and can still ride it, and it was worth it. The moral
of the story is obvious. What we're asking of you requires the same
process. The consequences -- that is, the stakes -- are much more serious. It is now life and health and promising potential versus probable
ruin of health, character, your potential contentedness, and even your
life and soul, Ben.

"You are welcome in our home. Kitty and I are wiping the slate
clean for you, but we will not be forgetting who you are or who you
have become, and we will be ever-vigilant to be aware of what you
are doing, to recognize the good that you do, but also any undesir-
able behavior, attitude, or comments. Our observations could bring
rewards or punishment. It is the nature of society and us to expect
you to continue your current behavior. We will hope otherwise. If you
give us your word, we will honor it, unless and until you break it and
we catch you lying, cheating, or deceiving us. If that occurs, we will
be intolerant. You will be grounded for the minutest infraction. You
will be lectured until you confess to understanding the consequences
of wrongdoing and believably espouse the benefits of the right way
to do things.

"You will be expected to follow all our house rules. Keep your
room neat; lived-in is okay, but neat. Clothes should be kept in their
appropriate places and trash disposed of properly. You will join us
for meals and help with household chores. We expect you to converse in an open and friendly manner and be willing to sit and talk
about yourself, your life, your friends, your dreams, your fears, and
whatever is on your mind or on our minds, for that matter. Don't be
alarmed -- we will not be unreasonable, but neither should you be.
For starters, you may go out once a week with selected friends for
approved activities. You may not smoke, drink, or use drugs, even on
outings. Of course, your parents may visit or pick you up for visits or
church at any time.

"Grounded, by the way, means no outings, no TV, no computer -- just books and one-on-one time with Kitty or me. You have to agree to our rules before you get a room and before you are allowed to unpack your bags. We don't have any way of predicting how long this will take, but we have signed on for the duration as long as you are willing and we see you trying.

"If we say it's over, there's no second chance. It's over when we say it's over. And Ben, you would need to go home or go somewhere. I'm not trying to be mean or punitive, but we're not your mama and daddy. We're relatives more willing to give you a chance than most of the world out there. However, for you to learn how to get along and cope in the world and not be killed, or imprisoned by the laws and rules and societal expectations that you disdain and ignore or break to live life your way, Aunt Kitty and I will need to be all of those things for you. You need to know we won't give you a pass, like your mama and daddy. We will give you more than society or the law. We will give you love, caring, and understanding. We will also give you punishment for infractions and we will give you the boot if necessary. If you threaten to leave or quit, that is breaking your contract and will be an automatic week of grounding."

"I've explained the seriousness of this opportunity to Ben," Thomas defended.

Sam further elucidated, "I don't doubt that. What I'm concerned about is Ben's sincerity and his determination. I'm not sure that he believes you anymore. You've been telling him this all his life. Maybe he thinks he's immune to regular rules of life. After all, you do keep bailing him out. We won't. Neither will judges. Better that he learns it here at home than in jail. We won't cover up for him like you do, Thomas. We will show him what he can expect from the world as it is. But, like I said, with caring and understanding and love -- not with intolerance, quick-tempered retribution, broken kneecaps, or worse."

"You make him sound like a gangster. He's a kid. He's gotten in with the wrong crowd." Parental denial seemed to be Thomas' strong suit.

"Thomas, you are in denial. Who's this wrong crowd? It's other kids, Thomas, just like Ben. Wake up. The police and jail time are one step behind them and gaining. The more you let them get away with, the more they think they can get away with. Before you realize it, they are doing petty theft and before long they're up to felonies and more prison time. And Thomas, that's probably after you're about bankrupt with all of your efforts to protect him, bailing him out and making excuses. You call his actions mistakes rather than crime. He feels exonerated. It doesn't work when there are no consequences. You should see that by now. And the sooner he learns, the better it is for him and everyone else."

"I guess you're right. It's just, well; basically Ben's a good kid. He's made some mistakes. I feel guilty that we've let him down."

"Thomas, listen to yourself, 'We've let him down.' You're blaming yourself and sharing the blame with Lauren. All the while you're minimizing Ben's part by characterizing his criminal activity as *mistakes,* as if he were totally innocent of conscious participation. He's not dumb; he knows what he's doing. He likes the excitement, the attention from his peers, the show of caring and support from you. He's not worried about himself or you. You've managed to make everything turn out fine for him. He can't believe you are being so inflexible now."

"Aren't you being too harsh on Dad?" Ben blurted out.

Both Thomas and Sam were surprised that Ben spoke. Ben had heard all he wanted to hear. He needed to rescue himself. Uncle Sam was painting too bleak a picture. He started with a disarming technique. "Dad, it's all right. Uncle Sam's right. Nobody ever spelled it out like that for me. If I don't get my act together, I'm toast. I guess I sort of knew it, but didn't want to admit it." Thomas began to relax and swell with gratitude and newfound pride.

"I'll have to 'suck it up,' be more responsible, get my grades up, quit sneaking out, and give up my friends with dope. I can do it, but I don't have to impose on Uncle Sam and Aunt Kitty. I'll just go home and do the right thing."

Thomas' eyes were now moist. "Son, I'm so proud of you. Sam, I can't thank you enough. I could never have convinced him. I owe you a lot. Thank you. Let me know if I can do anything for you."

Ben was breathing a sigh of relief until Sam spoke up. "Ben, I know what you're doing; your dad doesn't. He's feeling with his heart; he's not thinking with his head. He's heard you make similar convincing pleas before, but he's forgetting your failure to follow through in the past. He wants to believe you. I know better. He should, but he can't get beyond the guilt-ridden, parental gullibility. You would go home and be a model son as far as Thomas and Lauren could tell for about two weeks, then you'd begin your little slide back into your preferred ways. A spade's a spade, Thomas. You have to call them right. Ben, you may as well know right now how it's going to be if you're here. If you walk out that door now or if Thomas takes you out that door, that's your last chance here. And I predict your next chance will be in jail."

"You think you've got me figured out, don't you?" Ben was taking a different tack now. If he attacked Sam, Thomas would have to defend him and take him home, or Sam would become furious and refuse to take him in and he could go home with dad. Either way, he would win. "You think you know everything -- what gives you the right to lecture me and my dad? You think Peggy hung the moon, but you have to know you're no saint. You smoked until you got cancer."

"That's enough, Ben," Thomas admonished.

"No, it's not. He knew the risk and went ahead. If he didn't care about his own life, he should have protected his health for Peggy and Aunt Kitty. Where were all *his* pious intentions? Did he just save them all up to dump on me and you? Ha, ha. What a hypocrite!"

"You've said enough, Ben." Thomas was stern. "Get in the car. Uncle Sam, I'm terribly sorry and embarrassed. We won't trouble you longer."

Sam, noticeably calm, responded, "Thomas, I knew what I was getting into. Sit down, both of you. Ben's right in many respects, so let the devil have his due. We addicts are more similar than dissimilar. I hit Ben and you hard. Ben hit back, quicker and harder than I expected. He's defending his status quo and with good points. Notice he did not dispute anything I said. He simply attacked me, and with good logic. He made the mistake of using anger, making it easier for me to tune out what he was saying and just defend against the anger. I know that when he introduces anger, that he is uncertain of the merit of his argument. So, instead he hopes to win by force of emotion. If I subdue my anger, I will appear more rational and credible."

"Sure, Ben," Sam continued. "I knew smoking was harmful to my health. Early on, however, we did not know, and were thoroughly addicted before we knew. We stupidly rationalized that since we didn't know, somehow the danger would not apply to us. After all, we could not see inside our bodies or feel the insidious changes. Besides, if we got sick with cancer or whatever, we would have the doctors cut it out or otherwise fix it. For years I hid my cigarettes from family and they pretended not to notice. I was devious and they enabled me, much like what's going on with you and your mama and daddy.

"I did get cancer and had it cut out, and hope I'm cured. But I live every day wondering if and when it might come back. It's like daily Russian roulette with a death sentence. You're right that I was no saint. But the ignorance and stupidity of my youth continued into adulthood, and the consequences I have suffered are no reason to forsake what life I have left, or prematurely give up on today's youth who don't have to be ignorant or be allowed to continue acting stupid. If I spend the remainder of my life atoning for my waywardness, it won't be enough as far as I'm concerned. But Ben, if I get through to one person and truly make a difference, I'll be thankful. And it would be especially rewarding if it were you. You are family, young, and intelligent -- and have many years to enjoy freedom from addiction."

"The two of you have got me on a roller coaster. I'm identifying with you both." Thomas was pleading for more understanding, if not a resolution.

Sam was blunt, "That's because you're an addict, Thomas, even a recovering addict and a parent of an addict. Ben, I hope you don't turn tail and run from me and your problems. You need to face them and get them under control. We can help. Kitty and I are inviting you to stay with us. Give us and yourself a chance that you may never again have offered to you."

Ben knew that he had been bested by a master, but somehow it was actually okay. He sort of even hoped it might work. He felt that something inside had been piqued which he had not previously experienced. He was even stimulated by the back and forth banter. The caring Sam had shown came through with strength and authority, but unapologetically. It was too early for him to grasp that what he was feeling was respect, something he was unaccustomed to experiencing.

Thomas and Lauren drove home thinking maybe, just maybe, this would work for Ben.

Sam and Kitty, after retreating to their bedroom, felt safely isolated. Sam asked Kitty, "What the devil have I gotten us into?"

"It was our decision, Sam. That poor boy needs help. We're going to do all we can and pray it works."

CHAPTER 17

Building Rapport

THE MAGNITUDE OF friction among Sam, Kitty, and Ben was horrendous by anyone's standards. It exceeded even their most pessimistic admissions and doubts. However, Kitty stood by Sam as they faced each and every day and their challenges with Ben. They remained true to their word with Ben. They gave praise for compliance and thoughtfulness, but punishment for insolence, inconsiderateness, and breaking the rules set down at the beginning.

The very first morning Ben overslept and eventually came to the kitchen around ten o'clock. As he looked around, it was obvious that the kitchen was clean. He remembered the rule to be on time for meals, so despite being hungry he elected to say nothing.

Kitty noticed his puzzlement. "Ben, if you're looking for breakfast, you're too late. If you're hungry, you can find milk in the fridge and a Pop-Tart in the pantry. Leave the kitchen as clean as you found it. It's not going to be life as usual here, Ben. We won't enable inappropriate behavior. After this morning, if you miss a meal, there won't be a rescue snack. You will wait until the next meal."

This is going to be worse than I thought. It's like jail. The message was getting through to Ben, however. He kept that thought to himself. He opened the refrigerator and took out a Coke.

"Now Ben, you have to listen. Did I say Coke or milk? Coke is not breakfast food. You may have milk or water and a Pop-Tart or cereal that you will prepare yourself. It's not all that difficult. You just have to put your mind to it."

"You guys are going to be strict, huh?"

"You might think of it that way, but really it's to make sure that you get to experience the way most people live. You will find it to be healthier and more rewarding."

Again Ben thought to himself, *Y'all call this living? Your heads must be filled with nothing but friggin' rule books.*

"Good morning, Ben," Sam announced his entrance. "After lunch I'll be headed up to the lake to check on the boat and the house. I need to make sure everything's okay up there and perhaps I'll cut the grass. Care to go along with me?"

Ben thought, *You're trying to rope me into cutting grass, probably for free.* But he thought better of it. *I'd better play along. I'm not doing too well so far.* "Sure thing. What time do we leave?"

"Soon as we finish lunch. What time is lunch, honey?"

"Twelve o'clock."

"Super."

Driving to the lake was Sam's opportunity for one-on-one, man-to-man talk with Ben. "Kitty and I love you, Ben, enough to be tough on you. We will be like the Marines. Perhaps it is tough love, but hey, we want you to survive out there. So far, from what we're seeing, you're not likely to last very long in the real world.

You have the talent to be a leader, but you're a follower. And look who you're choosing to follow. Two of your friends have been kicked out of school. One has a DUI and a drug possession arrest. If I remember correctly, you had just gotten out of his car and he was on his way home. One has been to the hospital twice with an overdose. Look what happened to your own dad. Look what your early years were like before he cleaned up his act. Do you really want to waste your youth, all your life, living day to day with Russian roulette odds? No, I don't think so, Ben. What were your dreams and your goals before you got hooked into this vicious drug cycle?"

"Actually, Uncle Sam, I didn't have dreams. I was never encouraged to dream of the future. Potential was never a topic of discussion. We talked more about problems and getting by."

"You see Ben, that was the trap your dad got snared into, and it affected your entire family, including you. It discouraged you; it hindered you. But Ben, all that happened through osmosis to you. You were just in it, soaking it in. Your brain knows better than that, Ben. If you will be honest with yourself, you are smarter than that. Your dad has even wised up to being smarter than being a druggie. So come on man, don't wait as long as he did. Use your brain, man." Sam purposefully used and repeated the descriptor *man* instead of *boy*.

"I hear what you're saying and it makes good sense, it's just hard to see myself differently. Know what I mean?"

"Of course I know what you mean. It's like being in a parade out of uniform. Everyone looks at you funny. You're all thumbs, right?"

"Sort of like that. How did you know?"

"Been there, done that. All of us addicts do that when we change. It takes a while to learn to march to a new drummer. Eventually, we fit in. It's called comfortable recovery, or comfortable sobriety. It took me a long time to get there. I would reach for my pack of cigarettes, wake up wanting a cigarette, or see someone smoking one and want one for myself. But now I've been smoke-free for five years and, believe me, it does get easier with time. But it was over two years before I quit having strong cravings at times. And you know what? It took six months before I quit coughing up brown junk."

At the lake, Ben seemed more at ease and even proved helpful with the chores. Sam took this as another hopeful sign and gave Ben deserved compliments.

Ben adapted to the house rules, mainly to prevent being grounded, which he absolutely detested. He would question the reason or need for their rules and attempt to debate the issue, but he always lost. One example was on an earned outing. He wanted the usual curfew extended to a later hour. He pleaded that he was old enough to take care of himself. Sam and Kitty were firm. "It takes longer than a few weeks to rebuild squandered trust, Ben." He had to tolerate them, but he believed them to be entirely too cautious and unfair. Secretly, he was sure that he would be capable of returning to a controlled recreational use of his drugs without harm to himself or others. He was restless about staying with Sam and Kitty any longer. It had now been over two months and there had been no mention by them of his going home. As part of their original contract, however, he could not bring up the subject without incurring a week of grounding. It seemed they had thought of every possible rule to frustrate his tactics. Ben resolved to talk with his parents at the upcoming family reunion. He felt confident that they would believe him and if it were them talking to Uncle Sam and Aunt Kitty, they might agree to let him go home. At least he would not be grounded.

CHAPTER 18

Family Reunion

EILEEN ROBBINS, SAM'S niece, drove herself from Atlanta, Georgia to Decatur, Alabama arriving at the Amberly Suites Hotel at 3:30 p.m. local time after two hours of precious solitude garnered by driving alone. Driving kept her awake and alert, but left 90 percent of her brain available for mental gymnastics fun, concocting things to say and do during their family reunion. She rehearsed her plan, the sequencing of the events, so meticulously crafted. At 52, her penchant for organization and detail had remained a lifelong ally and had grown in importance, though it was perhaps a sometimes irritant to those around her. She had settled into a lifestyle that suited her personality. She filled her days with busy work, interesting things, and excitement. Dr. Lavoy had cautioned that she lived in a state of hypomania, consequently risking or flirting with another episode of mania or depression. He had even wanted her to increase her lithium, but she prevailed in her refusal. This was her personality, her norm, or her proclaimed euthymia, that she reasoned to be higher-functioning and better than the average. She did not want to be slowed any more, and generally abhorred the thought of having to work and play at the average person's usual pace; she would feel less than herself. Eileen had learned much of Lavoy's lingo and freely used it in conversation with him, "slowing would only make me feel *dysthymic* or *psychomotor retarded.*" She preferred the energized state, though realized the need to avoid mania. Her manic highs admittedly were addictive for her, but could be painful and devastating.

In less than an hour she had organized her suite to appear lived in and comfortable. She made sure it would be inviting for Robert and Wendell, their third child, when they would be driving over the following afternoon. They had waited in Atlanta for Wendell to get out of school, while Robert took the opportunity to work another day.

Wendell, now twelve years old, was the direct result of her being off of her medication and on a high during which she was "hell-bent" to have another child. She had invoked Freddie's, her late friend, admonition to have "as many children as you want." Robert's lack of enthusiasm could not prevail against Eileen's persistence. Fortunately, Wendell, after arriving, had managed to make a complete doting father out of Robert, who now had less desire to work and even less energy for sex.

Eileen plunged into the unnecessary but compulsive task of confirming the arrangements for the weekend. She wanted to see the meeting room where their dinner gathering would be held. She needed to personally speak to the chef. She even wanted to know how many rooms had been booked. She wanted assurance from the concierge that the charter bus service she had booked would be reliable.

Leaving the concierge's desk, she spotted Uncle Sam at the check-in counter. Aunt Kitty was with him, but who could the young man with him be? A teenage boy she couldn't recognize. Knowing his face was familiar, she was frustrated with herself, but it was useless; she could not place him.

"Hello, Uncle Sam. Hi, Aunt Kitty."

"Hello, Eileen. You remember your nephew, Benjamin. Thomas is letting us borrow him to carry our bags."

"Of course. Ben, how are you? And my, how you have grown and changed since I last saw you."

"Hi, Aunt Eileen. Good to see you. Thanks for putting this together," Ben said, quickly displaying his affability.

Eileen persuaded Sam to give her thirty minutes of private time while Kitty and Ben took things to their rooms. Ben actually would be checking in later with his parents.

"Peggy told me that you had really become an advocate for stamping out smoking and drinking. I think that's wonderful. I'm sorry about your illness and I hope that you're totally well."

"Thanks, me too. Actually, I do feel that I'm A-OK. Have to be positive, you know."

"Of course. My middle one, Darla, is a fourth year student at Vanderbilt. I know she's smoking cigarettes and drinking. I'm afraid for her because of the inherent dangers, but also because I don't know if she has my bipolar gene. Robert and I have tried to talk some sense into her, in fact, all our children. But they, especially Darla, will hear none of it. Her generation especially seems to insist it's an innocuous pastime and recreational. They will simply quit before it gets to be a problem. What do they expect, Uncle Sam? A warning light will come on, like check oil level or something?"

"I suppose so. Wouldn't it be nice if a risk gauge would light up warning 'danger level high'? Sadly, Eileen, we publish warning charts, but Darla and millions like her are in denial -- they don't or won't read, see, or hear the warnings, and by and large, just plain don't believe them. They feel it would be inconvenient knowledge."

"So what's a parent to do?"

"So far, no legal trouble with Darla?" Sam asked.

"Correct. I'm just worried about her. Where will it end? Will it be with a pickled liver? Or could it end with a pickled brain, you know, cirrhosis or alcoholic dementia? Or even cancer, like you had, Uncle Sam. It's so scary." Eileen was being graphic.

Sam said, "We called that the $64,000 question in the old days. Now, it's simply a rhetorical question. Parents ask it without expecting or getting an answer that's helpful. We've found ourselves giving platitudes of compassion, similar to what we would say to a friend who's lost a loved one."

Eileen voiced frustration, "The situation feels almost as hopeless. It's terrible. I've cried, prayed, pleaded, and withheld allowance. Nothing works."

Sam observed, "The young, especially, are full of invincibility and hedonism. It's a dangerous combination, analogous to testosterone and gasoline. It's so frustrating for them to be so unmanageable. We like to think we have some remote control over our kids. You know, raise them right and they'll stay right. But it's as if they're out of range -- or perhaps, more aptly, in an area where there's too much interference."

"That says it. She's out of my reach, literally and figuratively. So if you can come up with anything, I'll be so grateful. There has to be some way to reach these kids before they ruin themselves." Eileen was reaching for answers.

Sam felt impotent. He was full of sympathy, empathy, and desire to help, but he had nothing to offer. He felt humiliated and wondered what he would say to Lavoy. What would Lavoy do? Probably offer a stint in rehab. Of course, she would miss her graduation with her friends. She wouldn't go for that. She would be furious. The anger and backlash would push her deeper into denial and further away. There had to be something he could do, but what?

After Kitty was sleeping soundly, Sam remained wide awake psychologically beating up on himself. *Some mentor you are. All your research and big ideas and what could you offer Eileen or Darla? Nothing! A big fat zero.* He got out of bed and sat at the desk. It occurred to him that *'I'm being so negative. I need to be positive and think of something.*

What if it were Peggy or even Brian? I wouldn't wimp out. I'd come up with something. Darla liked Kitty and me. She loved Peggy, who was her very favorite babysitter. She's bound to have good memories of all of us. Maybe I'll go over to Vanderbilt and visit her and tell her some of the facts about smoking and drinking. Sure, like she'd be real happy with that. I've got it! I'll write a letter to her. That would be minimally intrusive, and in written form. It could be powerful and something that could be revisited, maybe in less rebellious moments. Besides, that would make me think and organize what I need to say. I'll do it now.'

Sam picked up the pen from the desk and started writing his letter to Darla on the hotel stationery.

CHAPTER **19**

Breakfast with Eileen

SAM'S EXCITEMENT OVER his letter to Darla refused to allow a lingering sleep. Before the sun was up, he was in the restaurant having coffee, talking with the waitress, reading the paper, and watching the door for Eileen. He hoped she would approve, but also he knew that he could count on her for competent editing.

Sam glanced around the room, but when he glanced out the window, quite an unexpected nostalgic emotion gripped him. *These are my roots. This is where Kitty and I had our dinner before our senior prom. I felt so lucky to be with her. She was so beautiful. I knew she would be my gorgeous bride.*

Sam surprised Eileen by calling out to her before her second foot came through the door. "Eileen, good morning. Come join me." He stood to greet her. After a brief, affectionate hug he assisted her with the chair, signaled to the waitress for service, and then sat down and retrieved the letter from his pocket.

"Last night I was consumed with wanting to help Darla and you. I had an idea that maybe a letter would be better received than a phone call or another awkward mom/daughter rehash of tired admonitions or sermons, as she is sure to see them."

"You are so right. 'Don't lecture me, Mother. I can take care of myself. I know what I'm doing. I'm 21 years old. I'll be all right, really.' Was I that way? I don't think I was. She's going to turn me gray.

I think a letter's an excellent idea. Is that it?"

"It is. I might have gotten carried away. It's a bit verbose. It's the first draft, of course. I'll need your input. We'll tweak it if you like it."

Eileen, not at all surprised by Sam's having immediately leaped into action, took the letter as if she had been expecting it. It was the kind of thing she would do as a natural follow-through for anyone in need. Beginning to read, she abruptly interrupted herself to say, "Thank you, Uncle Sam. This was very nice of you." She read more slowly than usual, even reading some lines a second time as if she were analyzing a treatise.

Sam, feeling satisfied with his effort, nevertheless waited impatiently for Eileen's response.

"You really put a lot of effort into this. Thank you. It's good. Do you think Darla will understand? It's like asking the immature to become instantly mature."

"Like asking the blind to see, as they say. I hope it's an appeal to her intelligence and to open her mind to adult, responsible behavior."

"Okay, but the message might need a stronger call to action. It's difficult to know how hard to push. I do like it and appreciate it. At least it's something new. Maybe it will get her attention."

"I'll rewrite it on personal stationery and tweak it a bit before I mail it. I'll need her address."

"Of course; I'll write it on the back of the first page here. Oh, is Peggy coming? It's been quite a while since I've seen her. Is she doing okay?"

"Yes, she's fine and that little Brian is as smart and handsome as they come. I guess he's just about as perfect a grandson as there could ever be. Kitty says I'm spoiling him, but really the little booger is spoiling me. He makes me feel ten feet tall. Grandkids are special. It's a unique bond. I'm sure some child psychologist has probably written a book about that."

"That's great. I look forward to the joys of grandparenting too, but I'll be patient. That's something I won't rush." She laughed perfunctorily.

"I understand. Your kids need to live their own timetable, not yours."

"Thank you. Would you mind sending me a copy of your final version? I have a friend whose son needs to read it."

"Sure, glad to." With that comment, Sam realized the letter to Darla, though personal, had to be a more universal message. *That's going to be a challenge.*

CHAPTER 20

Gossip

KITTY INVITED SAM to have lunch on the veranda. With his renewed attentiveness to her, this was tantamount to a command, which he lovingly accepted. She thought it a reasonable idea to speculate as to how the reunion might unfold and turn out.

Kitty reminisced, "I can't remember any significant family gathering since Peggy was about Brian's age. So much has happened since then. Eileen and Robert moved to Atlanta. Herschel and Rachel, now retired, chase grandchildren; spoil them, if you ask me. Rachel's so afraid one of them will have *that* gene and do something terrible. That's why she's gotten so active in NAMI [National Alliance on Mental Illness] and DBSA [Depression and Bipolar Support Alliance]. She wants to make sure that she knows every sign to watch for and takes every precaution with them. I think she's gone overboard.

"Thomas had his personal trip through hell and back; and now, he's having to go back through it with Ben. It is awful what drugs do to people! They really screw up whole families. Just think, we were never involved in drugs, yet here we are in Thomas and Ben's hell."

"It's addiction, honey," Sam opined. "It caught and hooked so many of us. My cancer was my -- excuse me, our -- hell. My addiction was *only* with cigarettes."

"Sam, are you going to talk about addiction tonight, at a family reunion?"

"Eileen did ask me if I would say a few words on the subject. After all, Ben is here with Thomas and Lauren. Robert is drinking too much. Darla is smoking and probably drinking. Trevor is gambling and out of control. Gracie is smoking, drinking, and probably screwing around. Kitty, honey, I hate to say it, but we may be Alabama's most dysfunctional family." Together Sam and Kitty had seemingly gotten all the "lowdown" on the entire family.

"No, sweetie. We just know each other. So many more are like us or worse. Many only hide their addictions."

"Maybe you're right. Dr. Lavoy says that many families with problems are able to keep them to themselves. They exert a great deal of energy to avoid the gossip mongers who, of course, would tarnish their community standing. People work hard for approval and will go to great lengths to preserve it.

"I have concluded that gossip is an addiction. It is for many an uncontrollable habit. By putting others down it produces a sense of a high or joy – perverse though it is. A minister was quoted as saying the number one addiction is approval. He is probably correct. We have known for a hundred years that if babies are not shown love and caring -- approval -- they fail to thrive because of marasmus, which is infant depression. We have heard entertainment performers say that they are addicted to the applause of the audience.

"So I'll add two more addictions: approval and gossip, which is a way of getting approval by proxy or subterfuge. Perhaps gossip is one of the most harmful addictions. It has been said that firearms can kill once, but a vicious tongue can wound or kill repeatedly."

"Sam Robbins," Kitty accused, "you're just obsessed. You think everything is addiction."

"I'm just thinking aloud, but it does make sense to me. It was just a spontaneous, unplanned thought. However, the answer might just be in the comment. Addiction is a way of getting high. Gossip gives a relative high by putting someone else lower. Engaging the emotion releases adrenaline and endorphins, especially if laughter is involved. It becomes a way of life, just as much as smoking or pain pills or alcohol."

"I never thought about gossip as an addiction," Kitty offered.

"I never thought about it either, but it is food for thought. It is everywhere and impossible to avoid. But we don't have to participate."

"In fact," Kitty emphasized, "we must not participate."

Sam and Kitty took advantage of the unscheduled afternoon and visited with relatives whom they saw less often.

CHAPTER 21

Family Dinner

SAM AND KITTY rested for half an hour and freshened up before changing clothes and going to the dining room. Eileen spotted them immediately and motioned them up front to sit at the table next to her, Robert, Herschel, Rachel, and Wendell, her youngest son. Sam and Kitty joined Peggy, her husband George, and Brian at their table next to Eileen.

Eileen thanked Sam again for his help. She complimented Kitty on how good she looked and what fond memories she had of babysitting Peggy. She commented that it was really neat that Peggy, in turn, had been able to babysit her own Darla, before they moved to Atlanta.

Eileen went from table to table greeting and welcoming each and every one and giving thanks for their support and for their being there for Mama Beth's 92nd birthday. Several would either comment on Mama Beth's longevity and remarkable agility, or more likely, would ask if Mama Beth would be telling any of her stories. Eileen always answered, "I've told her that without a story, she gets no birthday cake."

Thomas, Lauren, and Benjamin were at the same table as Trevor, who had lost his wife, Jennifer, to leukemia earlier. This birthday celebration might be hard on him. He had brought his seventeen-year-old daughter, Janet, and her best friend, Maxine.

Thomas, on seeing how Eileen was greeting and welcoming and

always a helper, had the realization that he had never apologized to Eileen for his treatment of her when she visited him during his fresh-man year at Auburn University. He now realized what a jerk he had been and how different his life would have been had he only listened. He would tell her later on; maybe tomorrow he could catch a private moment, but not tonight. That would be part of the required amends in the twelve-step program.

Sam leaned over and whispered to Kitty, "Eileen must be off her medicine. Look at her go. You'd think she was a politician."

Eileen took the podium and tapped her glass until she had every-one's attention. She asked for recognition of Mama Beth, their guest of honor, for her 92nd birthday. A hearty round of applause followed, prompting everyone to cheer except Mama Beth, who was visibly moved and appreciative.

"After we have ordered our dinner, Uncle Sam will tell us a little about his recent venture and passion, fighting addiction, and how it affected him, and probably most of us, and millions more. I had a chance to talk to him last evening and this morning and I find the whole subject very fascinating, so I asked him to share some of it with us tonight. He graciously consented and said he would, whether you wanted him to or not." This prompted a hearty round of laughs.

Eileen then gave instructions on where and when to meet for the US Space and Rocket Center on Saturday morning. She pointed out a couple of must-see exhibits, including the Saturn V moon rocket. She stated that the highlight of the reunion would be the birthday cel-ebration Saturday night banquet. Eileen wanted everyone to consider telling a personal story after dinner. She figured that would challenge Mama Beth to not be outdone.

Sam noticed Ben in lively conversation with Maxine, whom he was seated next to. Sam remembered when he was barely seventeen and had hormones more active than his brain.

Knowing Ben's history as he did, he was justified to worry. *Uh oh – this could be trouble. I hope Thomas is alert to what's happening.*

Eileen captured Sam's attention by calling his name and introducing him as Mama Beth's youngest boy. "If he had been a girl, that is if Daisy had come before Sam, there would be no Sam. Mama Beth kept having children until she could have at least one girl. So thanks for waiting, Daisy -- and Sam, you barely squeaked in. We're glad you did, by the way. Come on up and tell us about your crusade against addiction. I know it's very personal to you, and since you're family, it's personal to all of us as well."

"Thank you, Eileen. Most of you understand that she twisted my arm to get me to do this. I see at least one of you out there that I've not met, so here goes…

"Hello, my name is Sam Robbins and I'm an addict, much like many of you, whether you admit it or not, and many millions more as well. Why should I tell you my story and why should you listen or care? I'll tell you why. To learn from me what addiction did to me and it is waiting to do to you. But I'll also give you some useful knowledge that could save your life or the lives of your children and friends if you're willing to share this information with them."

Sam did not usurp the entire evening with his full lecture, but made sure they knew that each of them most likely had some addiction that they nurtured, whether it was smoking, like him, or some other dangerous or expensive addiction.

Within minutes, Trevor had maneuvered Sam off for a private conversation. He began by saying, "Sam, I can never repay you guys enough for taking me in. You know, I was only five years old when we had that car wreck and Mama and Daddy and my sister Trina, who was only eight years old, were killed. Aunt Beth took me in and raised me like I was one of you. I mostly called her Mama Beth just like the rest of the kids. She probably never told you, and I never talk about it, but I know my daddy was drunk when we had that accident. I'm sure grateful that he had a sister like Mama Beth. But Sam, the real reason I came over was to tell you that you woke me up tonight. I almost didn't come to this reunion. Now I know why I came. I've got a problem with gambling and thanks to you I see it now and I want to get help."

"It's funny," Trevor continued, "I dealt with addiction up close and personal with my wife, Jennifer, but never thought about it for myself. You know, when you're talking about it, you should mention intervention. That was the only way we ever got help for Jennifer. She had actually gotten into alcohol so badly that it was affecting our family. She was always irritable and fussing at Janet and me. Her drinking escalated dramatically when she learned that she had an incurable illness. She denied that she had a problem. Our doctor tried to talk to her. She refused to listen. He advised me to call Bradford, a substance abuse facility, and set up an intervention. I didn't know what intervention was. The counselors were excellent. They sent an intervention specialist and we set up a meeting, trapped her in her own house, and kept at her until she finally admitted she needed help and agreed to go for inpatient rehab. I'm just telling you this because you didn't mention intervention sessions when you were talking. Anyone with an addiction, who won't get help, needs to have an intervention. People will tell you that you can't help anybody unless they want to be helped and are willing, but I'm here to tell you intervention works."

"Thank you, Trevor. You are family and I'm honored to be your brother. I'm touched that I said something that might be helpful to you. I do strongly encourage you to check out Gambler's Anonymous and keep me posted if I can be of any further help."

Later, one by one, several of the family spoke to Sam, confessing in very similar sentiments; they had originally felt imposed upon to be subjected to his personal project, but admitted they had learned some useful information and were so glad he had spoken to them. To his surprise, a few even shared personal difficulties and sought more specific advice.

Sam was noticing a pattern. When a family member opened up and begins talking about addiction in their family, it was as if a huge dam had broken. A flood of emotions poured out including anger, resentment, helplessness, frustration, self doubt, guilt, sadness, pity, fear, distrust, shame, and being trapped. Most would use denial and their own attempts at rehabilitation techniques. For example, *We did all we could. We didn't recognize it in time. We tried everything.* Sam always reassured them that their story fit right in with other families in feeling blindsided. An unaffected family would find it very difficult to fully appreciate the devastation one addict can cause to a family.

The experience was gratifying to Sam. It would serve as a positive prompter if he was having doubts on whether or not to speak in the future when called upon in unscheduled opportunities.

CHAPTER 22

Huntsville Space Center

THE CHARTERED BUS accommodated all who had signed up for the US Space and Rocket Center, the enviable largest space and rocket museum in the world. The tour would also feature a two-hour visit to the George C. Marshall Space and Flight Center. Here the Saturn V Moon Rocket had been designed and developed, as well as the Lunar Rover "space buggy."

Sam noticed that Ben had managed to sit beside Maxine. He definitely planned to keep an eye on them.

Like an Orlando resident who never goes to Disney World, Sam had never visited Huntsville's Space Center and Museum. No matter, he was definitely proud of Alabama's leading role in space exploration. Eileen, on the other hand, had visited several times and was quite knowledgeable about the center. Even so, the enormity of the Saturn V never failed to impress her, or for that matter, most people who are fortunate enough to personally visit and see it for themselves. After all, it is the length of a football field and composed of at least five million separate pieces.

Sam took it all in, including the simulated spaceship journey, the Gemini capsule, the moon lander, the Mars Rover, the moon rock specimens on display, the Explorer (the first US satellite), and the Hubble Telescope. He did have the good sense to pass on the G-Force Accelerator, which spins its riders fast enough to exert three times the force of gravity. He likened the display of missiles used for space launches to a forest of metal limbless trees.

A visit to the shuttle was a very special treat. It offered an opportunity to reflect on the accomplishments it had facilitated, but also the lives lost in the exploration, particularly with the disasters of Challenger and Columbia.

Eileen's dreams to be a space explorer had settled into the reality of being a space buff. Occasionally, she would get the renewed inspiration to think her dream could still come true.

Space Day, as Eileen had called it for them, was full and busy. Sam, despite enjoying it, had felt relief when it was time to board the bus and head back to the hotel. Trying to be relaxed and enjoy himself, yet being a vigilant watchdog over Ben and Maxine, had been a strain on him. Several times he had spotted the two holding hands, but thankfully nothing more.

Sam could not remember visiting a more pleasant and yet educational tourist destination. Prior to the visit, he had been surprised to learn that more than 500,000 tourists per year make the Space Center a vacation destination. At the end of the day, he believed that number would grow as others learned about its offerings.

How neat, Sam thought, *that Alabama had a major role in the inaugural lunar mission, as well as other missions.* Sam remembered hearing a friend talking about things that had been invented or were first in Alabama. Chuckling inside, remembering that seamless hose and permanent press shirts had their beginning in Alabama. George Washington Carver won international fame with agricultural research and work on peanuts at Tuskegee Institute. Jesse Owens came from Oakville, Alabama to become America's first African-American to win a gold medal. Helen Keller, who overcame her own blindness and deafness to become an inspiration to others faced with difficult challenges; Harper Lee, who authored *To Kill a Mockingbird*; Nat "King" Cole, who was a leading jazz pianist and singer of several vocal hits -- they all were born in Alabama. His mind was recalling even more musicians, athletes, authors, and inventors from his state.

Sam had also noticed another inseparable couple for the entire day. Brian had taken a worshipful liking to Mama Beth. He stayed with her as if their hands had been glued together, parting just long enough to enjoy an ice cream cone and other goodies. They seemed to talk all day long. Every time he glanced at them, one of them seemed to be talking. He wondered which one of them would win a talking contest.

CHAPTER 23

Birthday Banquet

SPACE DAY HAD been Eileen's contrivance and her show. This evening, however, was Mama Beth's 92nd birthday banquet. Eileen had decorated everything with colorful flowers, balloons, and ribbons. She announced, "Mama Beth is the queen of the Robbins family and here is her tiara to prove it."

Eileen was the self-appointed and perfect greeter. She was able to say something pertinent to each and every person in the room. She asked them individually if any of them had a personal story they would like to tell, joking that someone needed to challenge Mama Beth. Everyone begged off until little Brian proudly announced that he had a story to tell and Mama Beth had helped him practice. Eileen was surprised. "So you had professional coaching. You will be tough competition."

Sam and Peggy were also surprised, as they immediately recognized it would be them on pins and needles, wondering if their secrets were at risk. Kitty and Peggy's husband, George, were quite nonchalant and it would appear they had no worries about secrets. They were excited.

Mama Beth came to their table and, to everyone's relief, revealed that Brian had shared his story about his fishing trip with Sam. She thought it was a wonderful story and encouraged him to tell it. "Th sooner one starts, the easier it is and someone has to c legacy. Sam, Brian couldn't remember the couple's name, but said the woman had been very nice to keep him warm and y'all paid him with your fish."

Sam laughed. "Well, we did actually did give them our one fish. Brian, they were Julia and Jim Goodson."

"Oh," Mama Beth said. "Brian, can you remember the names?" She knew she would not forget.

"I don't know. Can Papa come with me?"

At the same time, Mama Beth and Sam said, "Sure."

Mama Beth whispered something in Eileen's ear while being escorted to her table. Eileen went to the podium and tapped on a glass until she had everyone's attention. She announced that everyone should enjoy their meal and afterward there would be a storytelling contest.

"So far, only three have signed up, but if anyone else wants to tell a personal life story, let me know. The third and last story of the evening will be Mama Beth telling one of her stories. The second story will be Brian, son of Peggy and George Cummings, and grandson of Sam and Kitty, and great-grandson of Mama Beth who, we have just learned, has been coaching Brian on telling his story tonight. And number one will be me as I give you a short story about my visit to the psychiatric unit back in the '70s." She noted the stories would commence as soon as everyone had finished their dessert of Mama Beth's favorite, coconut cake and ice cream. For the storytelling, they would adjourn to the reception room.

After the meal, dessert was consumed with anxious haste. Mama Beth was the exception. Artful in building anticipation, she lingered and savored every bite as family members came by and wished her the happiest of birthdays and many more. She enjoyed the moment and the excitement. All mentioned being eager to hear one of her stories.

Mama Beth was the last to leave the banquet hall and enter the now rearranged reception room. When she entered, the applause was thunderous, and Eileen began leading them in singing "For She's a

Jolly Good Fellow." It had been years since Mama Beth had so sin-gularly felt honored, loved, recognized, and praised. Yet she had no anxiety about the crowd or her telling a story. She was professional at the art. Actually, she was as excited as anyone in the room. It was always fun to tell a story, particularly for the first time. This time, how-ever, was the most unique situation she had ever been in relative to telling a story. Portions would be things the audience had never heard and would be things that had just been revealed to her. She excitedly anticipated seeing their reactions as she recounted her story.

As the social hum began to subside, Eileen tapped the glass and told everyone, "I promised you two surprises before the evening was over. I'm not it. Our guest of honor herself, Mama Beth, is our sur-prise. She has just informed me that she is going to tell us a story that she has never told before, so we are in for a treat. Most of us have heard her telling stories and know her abilities. Some of us may have never been privileged to hear one of her stories. Janet has heard her stories, been thrilled by them, and personally challenged to write about her own stories. She can take credit for talking Mama Beth into telling us one of her stories tonight. Mama Beth tells me we're going to be surprised. So, we'll be listening closely, Mama Beth."

"But first, my story." Eileen recounted for them some of her ex-perience of being on the psychiatric unit in the '70s -- what she had observed, how she had felt, the awakening she had experienced -- but before taking up too much time, simply stated that they could get the rest of the story by reading the book about her, *Fly Me to the Moon*.

Eileen then introduced Brian. She motioned for Brian to come to the podium. Brian took his Papa Sam's hand and confidently walked to where Eileen stood. She positioned him so that he could speak into the microphone.

Sam looked out at the audience and gave a shoulder shrug as if to say, "This is new to me; I'm puzzled," which was translated into "Actually, I'm nervous about what to expect." Soft laughter rippled through the room, in understanding of his peculiar position. Sam looked out and saw Mama Beth encouraging Brian to speak up.

"My Papa took me fishing, only we went swimming too. We got up real early and I was *so* sleepy. Papa was really happy, so I got happy too. I had to help him load the boat and we went way out on this big lake. Papa was going to teach me to fish. Nobody else likes to fish. We were out there all by ourselves. Papa showed me how to fish. He went to the other end of the boat. I caught a fish that was so big it pulled me into the lake. I couldn't see a thing. I didn't know what to do. After a long time, I thought the fish got me, but it was my Papa. He was kicking and jerking real hard. I couldn't breathe and I was really cold. And then this lady and man pulled us up out of the water and into their boat. What's their name, Papa?"

"Julia and Jim Goodson."

"Right, Miss Julia. She wrapped me up and held me real close 'til I was warm again. Papa got the fish and gave it to them. They were real nice. Then we went home. The End."

The room erupted with applause and whistles and encouraging shouts of "Great!"

Beaming, Brian took Papa Sam's hand and they went to their table. Sam was looking at Peggy and wondering how much she had learned that she didn't already know.

"Well, Mama Beth, you might have prematurely over-trained your replacement. Thank you, Brian; that was wonderful. But even though you beat me, don't be disappointed if Mama Beth surprises us all like she always does. By the way, Mama Beth, I want to bring my tape recorder and spend about a week with you. Your stories need to be recorded."

Defying her age, Mama Beth walked spryly to the podium and announced that spontaneity was sometimes better than rehearsed or repeated stories. So tonight, she decided to take a chance and tell a story she had never told before. She begged their indulgence, therefore, as she offered unrehearsed memories from long past, and some new insights.

CHAPTER **24**

What Goes Around, Comes Around

MAMA BETH WAS introduced by Eileen as if no one knew who she was. "Here stands before you the wellspring of your genetic strengths, and North Alabama's greatest storyteller. Brace yourselves. Personally, I can't wait. Mama Beth, take it away."

This was the story Mama Beth told:

Well, my goodness gracious, nobody ever made such a fuss over me before except maybe John Paul, God rest his soul. I probably never mentioned it before, but you know, I thought he would never notice me. I tried every flirtatious trick that a fifteen-year-old could know, but he would always act blind. I knew I was not bad-looking, and some even said I was beautiful. Oh, those were the days.

Back then, we walked almost everywhere we went. One fateful day, I walked about a quarter mile up to Yancey's general store to get a quart of kerosene for our lamp. When I saw John Paul there, I turned red as a beet that was grown on top of Iron Mountain. I probably looked more like an Indian. John Paul was by himself, so there were no fellers there to tease him.

"Hi," he said. I noticed a little nervous quiver in his voice. My pulse rate went up. I had been noticed. Life would never be the same after that. I wished I had been wearing something prettier, but soon realized it was me he was looking at – eye to eye – not my clothes.

He offered me a drink, a Royal Crown cola, and then he walked me home, opposite the direction of his house. I knew that day I was going to marry John Paul and I think he knew it too, and that's how this entire family got started. But that's not the new story I wanted to tell.

I want to tell you Mama Beth's version of what goes around, comes around. After Sam was born, old man fate put his finger on me in quite an unexpected way. Sam thrived and gave me no problems. When he was about a year and maybe a half, I had a strange visit from the sheriff.

"Hello, Sheriff. What brings you to my door? If you're looking for moonshine, we don't have any of that around here."

"Of course not, Miss Bethany. I'm on a mercy mission. You know that girl Wilma Jean had her baby boy two weeks ago. Well, her milk ain't come down yet. They've been keeping him alive with sugar water, but Miss Bethany, he can't hold on much longer. It would be shameful to let him starve, and little Sam -- well, he's doing real good now. We were wondering…"

"Sheriff," I said to him, "is that the little girl that's not married?"

"Yes ma'am, it is, Miss Bethany. But she's eighteen years old and the boy that's the father tried to marry her over a year ago. Her Pappy wouldn't let 'em marry because he didn't like him because, you know, he had a run-in with the boy's dad years ago when he was drinking. A more stubborn man I never saw. Now this poor girl is in an awful mess and I just know it's because she's afraid of her Pappy that her milk won't come down."

"Sheriff, that's awful. What is it you're asking?"

"Little Sam's going to be weaned soon, Miss Bethany. He's already eating pretty well, so if you could see your way clear to feed that little baby 'til he can eat on his own, you know, we'd be mighty grateful."

"Now Sheriff," I said, "are you sure about this girl and the boy? I've never been a wet nurse to any babies except my own. I just don't want to get tangled up with some tramp of a girl. My name would be mud in this little town."

"Yes, ma'am. I understand, but she is a fine girl and I know she's going to be a fine mother and a good wife, soon as old Luther lets her and my son get married. You see, he's been in love with her for two years and that's his son that's about to starve."

"Well, why didn't you say so, Sheriff? What do we do next?"

"Oh thank you, thank you. May the Lord bless you, Miss Bethany. There are some things you have to know and do. First of all, in this county we deputize wet nurses."

"Why in tarnation do I need to be deputized to nurse a baby?"

"It's not for feeding purposes, it's for protection, ma'am."

"Protection? Why would I need protection?"

"It's quite a walk from your place to hers. And since you'll make that walk many times and often alone and sometimes in the dark of night, there is the possibility that you could face danger -- a bear, or more likely a drunk crazed with the need of a woman." The sheriff continued, "You need to know, there are rules for things like this and all men know the rules and all wet nurses are honor bound to do everything in their power to supply their babies with the milk of life. You have to carry a double-barrel sawed-off shotgun. You have to keep it loaded and at the ready. You have to wear a white bonnet, so there will be no mistaking who you are.

"When you're going to the baby's house and you meet a man, even one you know, he is to move to the other side of the street. If he doesn't, you must stop. If he comes within fifteen feet of you, point the shotgun at his chest. You don't need to say a word. You don't want him to know if you're nervous. If he approaches you, whether polite or drunk, take no chances. Pull the trigger. If necessary, the second barrel too, then immediately reload. Always carry extra shells with you. Keep them in easy reach. Then you walk around him and go feed the baby."

"Are you serious?"

"Yes ma'am. In fact, it's never happened in this county, but I promise you it happens all the time. I hear about men being found in the morning lying in a pool of their own blood -- mostly drunks, who are only missed by the saloon keepers."

"I have heard of such things, but not around here, I just wasn't aware."

"I'm glad you're not, but now you know. It is a well-established custom. Miss Bethany, I brought you a white bonnet and a sawed-off shotgun, hoping you'd say yes. Can I walk out back with you and show you how to use it? It can have quite a little kick, and you need to know what to expect."

When I fired that thing, I never heard such a loud racket and I thought it was going to jump out of my hand. I prayed to God I would never have to fire it again. But one night, coming back from a midnight feeding, the streets were dark and lonely, my task was done, and I was tired and not too observant. Suddenly, there was a man right in front of me, maybe just six feet. It felt like my heart jumped up in my throat.

I raised the gun and shouted, "Get back!" He just looked at me.

Finally, he said, "You're taking care of that bastard baby and now you're going to take care of me." I was so afraid I couldn't even think straight. I didn't know the man, but I knew what he wanted. For the first time I was thankful that I had the shotgun, and I had it pointed right at his chest. He was drunk enough and crazy enough to take one last step toward me. The first barrel blasted off, ripping his chest open, picking him up off the ground and knocking him backward, flat on his back. He never even twitched or moved.

I forgot to reload the empty barrel. I guess I walked home; I don't remember. I didn't wake anybody at home, but I stayed up all night, reading my Bible and praying. At daybreak, it was time for another feeding. I reloaded, donned my white bonnet, and went on my trek for the six o'clock feeding, taking a slightly different route.

The feeding went routine. What Wilma Jean had not yet heard and I did not know was that her Pappy died around midnight the night before of a close-range shotgun blast to the chest. No one blamed me, but I blamed myself.

What we all learned later was that he was a frequent binge alcoholic and wife beater. Their marriage had been unhappy for years. His wife would be happier without him, especially now that her grandson could be part of her life. Furthermore, he had been abusive to Wilma Jean. Now you see, what goes around comes around.

There is more to the story. I had a real hard time with having taken a life, and I prayed every day of my life, even this morning, for a sign from God that it was okay. Pastor Grimes told me it was all right and I shouldn't worry about it. I did what had to be done. But still, it just didn't sit right – killing somebody. Our Sheriff's son, Raymond, and Wilma Jean were married and they raised the baby to be a fine young man. In fact, he was just a couple grades behind Sam in school. They knew each other, but not very well. Like Sam, he married his high school sweetheart and moved to Birmingham. But I didn't know until today that they had rekindled their acquaintance in the Birmingham area, having both bought a lake house on Smith Lake. You see, that Sheriff's name was Goodson and his son, Raymond, was the father of Jim Goodson, Julia's husband.

Mama Beth was looking directly at Sam and so was everyone else. Sam now was crying.

Mama Beth said, "You know, I've been afraid to die all these years because I didn't know until today that God understood. But He let me save that little baby's life, even though I took one; and then He let that little baby grow up and save the lives of my son, Sam, and my precious great-grandson, Brian. This is the best birthday gift I could ever have. So you see, the moral of the story is when you're faced with tough decisions, do the right thing. And what goes around will come around."

Contrary to the end of her usual stories, rather than applause the room was respectfully stunned into silence, emotionally drained.

Eileen eventually began what turned out to be an entertainer's *three curtain call* applause.

CHAPTER **25**

Winding Up

AFTER HEARING HOW Mama Beth saved Jim Goodson's life and that he grew up to save Sam's life, Sam sat sobbing more emotionally than Kitty could ever remember seeing him. The entire weekend had been a bit much for Sam. Kitty leaned over and whispered to Peggy, "I don't think your dad can take much more."

"Mr. Sam," a voice invaded their table. "May I call you Uncle Sam?" It was Maxine; Ben and Janet were with her. "I know you're Janet's uncle, but I want to claim you too. Ben told me what you're doing for him and I think that's so wonderful. He's such a nice boy. I really have gotten to like him. I just know he's going to be all right. Oh, and me too. I've been smoking a little, but no more, not after hearing you talk. You made me think how stupid smoking is. I'm stopping. My mama will be so proud. I can't wait to tell her about you and Ben and show her my bracelet that Ben bought for me. See?"

Sam's eyes quickly went to Maxine's raised left wrist and the impressive bracelet of gold and three pretty opal stones. Sam, though shocked, was quickly refocused by the chorus from the table of "how beautiful!" Sam commented, "Wow, you really must have impressed Benjamin."

"She's the nicest girl I've ever met," Ben was glad to opine. He had become so engrossed with Maxine that he forgot about enlisting his parents' aid to end his exile to Sam and Kitty's house.

Sam thanked Maxine for her kind words. He said he would be flattered to be her honorary uncle, admonished her to never slip back, and to spread the word: ban the stupidity and embrace life and health.

Sam then forced himself to stand tall and go over to Mama Beth, where he embraced her. He was unable to hold back tears as he cried openly. Mama Beth was also crying. Others began to cry and some began to move away. The contagion captured several as they collected into one huge embracing group, some sensing that this could well be their last hug with Mama Beth.

As Sam and Kitty returned to their room, Sam was grateful for his luck in having Kitty to console and comfort him in times like this. She obliged without his asking.

At breakfast, everyone was in a festive mood: handshaking, hugs -- some warm and tight, others more casual -- everyone promising to keep in touch and do this again soon.

Someone made a point of having to check out and get on the road. As if the retreat had sounded, inexplicably everyone was on their feet, waving their hurried goodbyes. The idea of a guided tour of the area had been abandoned.

Eileen kissed Robert and Wendell and sent them on their way. She stayed with Mama Beth and Daisy until they were packed. She assisted them to checkout, where they were told their charges were already paid. She didn't tell them it was her, only that it was the family's wishes and gratitude.

On Eileen's drive back to Atlanta, she contemplated Sam's letter to Darla and prayed for Sam and Darla as well.

Eileen had gotten Mama Beth to agree to a long visit and a marathon of telling as many stories as she could remember. Eileen would use her vacation days. She was not, however, feeling any sense of urgency for this.

CHAPTER 26

The Turn

THE FIRST WEEK after the reunion Sam felt validated, appreciated, and uncommonly content. He vowed to call Jim and Julia Goodson and for him and Kitty to have them over for dinner. He couldn't wait to share what he had learned from Mama Beth's story, but would not do it on the phone. He remembered promising Dr. Lavoy to provide him with one of Mama Beth's stories. He now had the perfect one to share.

Sam gave a copy of the draft letter to Darla to Dr. Lavoy and to Judith Vercher, LMFT, LPC -- a respected counselor friend and English perfectionist -- for their proofreading. He was now contemplating posting it on the Internet, but of course, not until after Darla had some private time with it.

On Friday, Sam picked up a 5 X 6 plaque, ordered on Tuesday, which read "Mama Beth Storytelling Merit Award to Brian Cummings, for My Fishing Trip." He called Peggy to alert her of his imminent visit.

Brian, always happy to see his Papa, was ecstatic with his plaque. This was his first official certificate of recognition, except for his diploma from kindergarten. He wanted his mom to read it to him even though Sam had already read it. Sam boasted and bragged about Brian's public speaking ability.

Kitty took the opportunity to ask if she now knew the whole picture of their fishing trip. Sam, trapped, filled her in on the details, admitting his fears -- even that they both might die. He admitted that after they were rescued, he was afraid she might not allow him to have further unsupervised visits.

"I really am glad I didn't know it all back then. It was easier on me this way."

"Me too," Sam allowed.

Ben had been on his best behavior with a pleasant attitude this week. Actually, it seemed, looking back, that he had improved over the several weeks he had been with them. He had adjusted to their routine and rules and they were cautiously optimistic about his recovery.

That evening, as Sam and Kitty dressed for a dinner outing, Kitty became anxious and was frantically looking everywhere, finally saying, "Sam, I can't find my pearl necklace. You know, the three-strand one that you gave me on our 30th anniversary."

"Maybe they're just misplaced, dear."

"You don't understand. One doesn't misplace something like that."

"Oh, me." Sam was already thinking, *Ben has snookered us*.

"Sam, it couldn't be Beulah, she's been housekeeping for us for fifteen years with never a single thing out of place or missing."

"I know. God, I hate this. Let's do our dinner thing. I'll call Thomas in the morning and let him know that I'm going to confront Ben. This may be the end of the line for him."

Their evening was spoiled. Conversation was a mixture of half-attention shared with anger, sorrow, pity, and dread of tomorrow.

Sleep that night was no better. Kitty, surprisingly, slept better than Sam. He was restless. He kept waking up, trying to figure out what to do and how to approach Ben and even Thomas, for that matter. It seemed, even in his sleep, he lamented his failure with Ben and a certain poor destiny for him that Sam had been increasingly convinced they were averting.

Around 4:00 a.m., Sam consoled himself with the thought, *This is not your fault. It never was your battle. You gave it your all. I must have the wisdom to know what I can do and what I can't do. Have I not done my best? What else can I do? Can I have a little help here?* Sam fell asleep.

When Sam woke up, Kitty was cooking cheese grits, eggs, bacon, and toast. The preserves and jams were already on the table and coffee was made. It had become a Saturday morning ritual to break from their low-carb, low-fat general diet. Sam poured a cup of coffee, greeted Kitty lovingly, and walked onto the back patio for solitude with nature. He loved a good cup of coffee in the morning and to watch the birds cheerfully going about their morning. Kitty knew this meant he needed no distraction by her conversation. He needed to fully charge his courage and determination to do what had to be done.

Ben came into the kitchen earlier than usual. He talked of how good breakfast smelled and asked where Uncle Sam was. Kitty became anxious now and wished Sam was in there. "You know, Aunt Kitty, I've been thinking this week."

Sam spotted Ben through the window and, worried that Kitty might say something, rushed into the kitchen asking if he was missing breakfast.

"No," Kitty informed him. "Ben was just telling me he had been thinking this week."

"Yes, ma'am, I've been thinking about everything all week. Last night I got a phone call that shook me up. My friend Vaughn died night before last. His mama found him dead on the floor yesterday morning. They think it was cocaine and alcohol. He is the second person I know who died on drugs."

"I'm sorry about Vaughn. It's really scary that you could be number three." Sam was blunt. He didn't have much sympathy for Ben at the moment.

"But I don't want to be number three. I want to live. Like I was telling Aunt Kitty, I've been thinking all week. I was trying to remember all the things you have told me. I remember how Vaughn sassed his parents; he called them names and he wouldn't obey them. He stole from them. They let him get away with it. I know I was starting to be like him. You said they were in trouble and if they didn't change, they would wind up in prison or dead. You told me that I would also. It didn't scare me then, but it does now.

"I've also been thinking about Maxine. You see, I really like Maxine. She's the nicest girl I've ever met. At first, I didn't tell her about my problems, but I finally did and I told her that y'all are helping me. What she told me made sense. She said, 'Your past is not what's important; it's what you do with your future.' That's what y'all have been saying too, right?

"Maxine said I could write her and see her again, but I was afraid I wasn't good enough for her, or her mom would refuse to let me see her. I gave her that bracelet sort of like trying to hold onto her by the wrist, you know, and not let her go. I thought it would make her like me more."

Even though breakfast was now on the table and everyone was seated, Ben paused only for the blessing and then kept talking.

"But like I said, I've been thinking this week, Maxine liked me before I gave her the bracelet. She would be happy that I spent it on her instead of drugs, which is what I had planned to spend it on. You see, I'm ashamed of it. I thought when I was out, you wouldn't know it if I used drugs, and so it really wouldn't matter. I figured nobody would know, so no one would be hurt. But then all those things you've been saying were actually true -- about who I am and my future and all. Maxine wouldn't have given me a second look or even a hello if she'd known about my drugs and my plan to use the first chance I got."

By then, Sam and Kitty were having quite similar thoughts. *What a con-artist. He's painting himself as already reformed. He thinks we don't know yet, so when we find out it will be too late because a reformed person surely would not steal from their gracious hosts. What a crock,* Sam thought. *When he's finished I will lower the boom on him, even though I haven't called Thomas yet.*

"Anyway, what Maxine said about the future really made me

think. I listened to what she said and I saw what she did. When she heard what you said about smoking and addiction, she quit right then and there. I know she means it. That impresses me. She asked me for my word that I'd stay quit. I gave it to her, but I didn't mean it at the time. It was later when I thought about being with her and what she said about the future, that made me think of all you've told me and how nice it is here with you. I would rather have this kind of life with Maxine than the life I have known. My chances for that actually do depend on choices I make now. You are giving me a second chance; Maxine's given me a second chance; Mom and Dad have given me one last chance. I'm better doing it your way. I want you to know I'm changing. I'm going to keep my word to Maxine. I'm through with drugs. I can do it and I will.

"If Maxine knew how I got that money, she would never see me again. That's really what I needed to talk to you about. I thought I could blow some smoke with you for a few weeks and pull the wool over your eyes, and by then Mom and Dad would be ready for me to come home, so I did play along. About two weeks ago, I did the worst thing I've ever done. I went into Aunt Kitty's jewelry case and took her pearl necklace and a diamond necklace and I pawned them. I got four hundred dollars. I planned to have a lot of fun with it. I spent most of it on that bracelet for Maxine, and some sodas. All I've got left is fifty dollars -- and here it is. I'm going to pay back the rest. I'll have to get a job. I don't want Maxine to know. Can you forgive me? Will you give me time to pay you back?"

Sam was in disbelief. Nobody would have confessed to such a crime unless they were genuine. However, he had to make very sure that Ben felt the entire profundity of his actions. Then he could have some leniency for his proactive confession.

"What you have just done takes a lot of courage and comes just in time, Ben. I was planning to call the sheriff right after breakfast this morning. I was going to have you arrested for grand larceny, a felony that would hang over you the rest of your entire life. It would strip you of voting rights and gun rights, and make getting a decent job nearly impossible. You were 30 minutes from prison, Ben."

"I didn't know you knew."

"You youngsters think we're old fogies and don't know what's going on. We knew you couldn't afford that bracelet. Deductive reasoning's not that difficult, Ben. The tough thing was deciding to send you to prison and bringing embarrassment on the family, but then we figured maybe prison could do for you what we had not been able to do. It might just save your life. Maybe you've come to your senses just in time."

"I know it will take me a long time to pay back four hundred dollars, but I'll do it."

"Ben, that jewelry was worth between five and ten thousand dollars. That's what you'll have to pay back. But even more, the sentimental value was priceless. That's irreplaceable."

"Oh my gosh, really?"

"Really, but maybe we can retrieve it. We'll take the receipt and go to the pawn shop and get it. You'll just have to pay back what it costs us to get it out of hock."

"I threw the receipt away. I was afraid you would find it."

"You're grounded -- no phone, no Internet, no nothing but talk. No visitors, no leaving the house. Get dressed. We're going to the pawn shop."

Sam waited until after 9:00 so the sheriff's office would be open. He would plan to dial that number first and then he would dial his attorney, Mr. Steele.

Sam had Ben to identify the pawnbroker through the window before they entered.

"Good morning," Sam started out. "This underage lad is my nephew. He brought goods in here a couple of weeks ago without our permission and pawned them to you for four hundred dollars. We're here to retrieve them. If you will kindly pull them so we can inspect them and redeem them."

"Sure, if I can have the receipt, please."

"Well, the kid figured since you and he were dealing in stolen goods, it might be best to lose the receipt. But if you've forgotten I can refresh your memory. It's a three-string pearl necklace and a beautiful diamond necklace."

"I'm sorry, but without a receipt, there's nothing I can do."

Sam took out his cell phone and a piece of paper. "This first phone number is the sheriff's office. I'll call my friend there. Would a search warrant be adequate as substitute for a receipt? The second call will be to my lawyer to sue you. You never asked for this boy's age or anything. You knew it was stolen property. I'll have you jailed and your place closed."

"Could you give me a moment, please? I'll see if I can locate them."

"Only if I can accompany you every step of the way."

"That won't be necessary."

"Maybe not for you, but for me, it's necessary."

"Very well."

The items were quickly located and brought back to the counter. "I believe you will find them in excellent condition, sir. Do you wish to claim them?"

"Yes, thank you."

"Very well, that will be five hundred dollars."

"You only gave him four hundred dollars."

"True, but the interest…"

"Will be zero, under the circumstances. And you're mighty lucky the police aren't already at your door. Here's four hundred dollars. Give me a paid in full receipt, which I definitely will not lose."

The pawnbroker obliged. Sam took the receipt and the jewelry and left with Ben following closely.

In the car driving home, Ben was quiet. Sam finally broke the silence. "I would've turned him in, but then you too would have been involved. But Ben, somewhere along the way you won't have someone protecting you. This time you must make good on your promises to get your life on the right track. I seriously doubt that you will have another chance."

"I will, I have, I mean….That was awesome, what you did. Why did you go in the back with him? Were you afraid he would run?"

"Perhaps, or call friends to come outnumber us. Taking chances can get you killed, Ben."

Kitty was thrilled beyond description to get her prized jewelry back.

Sam, feeling understandably bolstered, retreated to his study where he retrieved his letter to Darla, which was now tweaked with the contributions from Lavoy and Judith Vercher. He carefully reconstructed it into final form so that he could send it on to Eileen in a stand alone form. If she approved the final form, he would send it along to Darla. Later, he would post it on the Internet, but with a fictitious name.

CHAPTER 27

Chance Encounter

BY CHANCE, SAM encountered Brent Shotlan in the parking lot of his favorite home improvement store. Brent had been Sam's foreman for several years before alcohol ruined his life. Sam had agonized over terminating Brent because he personally liked him and knew that he had a wife and three children. Brent had made several mistakes at work, which had been costly to Sam and the company. Sam knew that these mistakes were related to Brent's drinking. Yet he had tolerated them until one final mistake was the last straw. It cost the company fifteen thousand dollars and an ugly PR result. "Brent," Sam had said, "how could you let that stuff ruin you? You've been my best foreman for years; now you're my worst employee. I have tried everything I know to get you to go for help, but now you're ruining my company. I've got to let you go. I'm sorry, but this is your last day. Please pick up your things and leave the premises. Your insurance is good until the first of the month. That's three weeks. I strongly advise you to go get help. I can't take you back after this, but you're just in your forties, so you could still have a good life. I truly wish you well, Brent. I'm sorry."

Sam had later heard that Brent only went deeper into the bottle, losing his wife and children and eventually going bankrupt. He hardly knew whether to speak or not. Brent solved his dilemma.

"Hi, Mr. Robbins. How are you?"

"Hi, Brent. I'm fine. How are you?" Sam asked with genuine interest.

"I'm okay. I finally got that help you kept telling me to get. I'm working the steps and I need to apologize to you. I hope you will accept my apology, but there's no way that I can make restitution to you for the grief and the expense I caused you; I'm sorry. I'm truly sorry."

"I greatly appreciate that, Brent. It means a lot to me. You know how much it hurt me to let you go."

"If you had not turned me loose, I would have hurt you worse and might have drunk myself to death. I lost everything and eventually took an overdose and almost died. I was admitted to a hospital; then I was detoxed and nourished and pumped up. I thought I had it licked. But I began easing back into it. And then before I realized it, I was drowning in booze again. I got into Bradford's rehabilitation treatment program and stayed there a month. They took away all my cockiness. They finally made me see that it wasn't everyone else's problem. It was my problem. Now I'm actually fighting it much harder than ever before."

"That's good to hear, Brent. As you were talking it dawned on me how similar we are. I've learned a lot these past few years. You see, I'm an addict also. Mine was cigarettes. You knew, but didn't tell me to get help. And if you had, like so many others, I would have ignored you just like you ignored me. I might have even told you to mind your own business; it's my body and I can do with it as I wish.

"You and I were like heavy locomotives on different stupid paths and nothing was going to deter us. I finally stopped smoking, but it was too late. I still got lung cancer."

"Oh my, Mr. Robbins! I had not heard. Are you all right?"

"I think so. At least so far, so good. But that's not all. I probably influenced others to smoke, maybe even enabled them…"

Interrupting, Brent said, "Like you enabled me? I'm sorry. That was inappropriate and unfair. Forgive me. I apologize."

"No, you're quite right. Hindsight's easier for most of us. I'm trying to make up for my past. I've got this campaign going, sort of a war on addictions. All addictions. Right now my nephew's living with me.

He's so screwed up. He's got multiple addictions. Plus, he thinks he knows it all and we're just old fuddy-duddies."

"Been there, done that. Bet he thinks you don't know crap about addiction. Hey, what's just cigarettes when he's into the hard stuff, right?"

"That's about it. I think we're making progress and then he does something so stupid that it makes me feel downright naïve. I'm really scared for that boy. Lately he's telling me that he's seen the light and he's going to be okay, but I'm still skeptical."

"Hey, bring him to one of our AA meetings. I can say some pointed things to him. You never know what will hit home. I have to say though, in a million years, I would never have thought of us being similar with addictions."

"I know. Most people don't. But addiction is addiction. That's what I've come to believe and I'm determined to get the word out. Knowledge is power. Forewarned is forearmed. People need to know what they're facing and how to save themselves and their families from all these addictions. When do you guys meet? I'll definitely bring Ben."

Sam and Brent found a mutually acceptable AA meeting date.

CHAPTER 28

AA Meeting

SAM APPROACHED BEN with enthusiasm. He explained that they were going to an AA meeting. He especially wanted Ben to hear from others what addiction had done to them. It would be different and perhaps more meaningful to hear from others as opposed to hearing just from Sam and Ben's dad. Purposefully, he ignored mentioning Brent, hoping to avoid being accused of planning a conspiracy.

Ben, wise now to responses resulting in disappointment and therefore disapproval from Sam, rather quickly offered a semi-warm response. He knew that feigned enthusiasm would backfire. "Well, that should be interesting. You did say that you will go with me, right? I would feel, you know, funny, showing up there by myself."

"Sure, Doc says a few of these meetings will open my eyes, so I might as well go along. Besides, don't forget, I'm also an addict." Secretly Sam was hoping they would hear some of the horror stories that Dr. Lavoy had shared with him. He wanted to scare Ben with them, but had not found an opportune time to bring them up.

Although Ben was anxious on the evening of the meeting, he expected to waste the night. *What can a drunk teach me?* He doubted he would even listen to much of what was said. It was not his idea of entertainment or classwork.

Introductions were made as they entered, using first names only. When Brent introduced himself, it was as nonchalant as any of the other introductions, but he did sneak a wink to Sam.

Eventually the first person to speak broke the chatter with an announcement.

"Y'all give me your attention, please. My name is Virgil and I'm an alcoholic. I was taken over by alcohol by the time I reached 25 years old. I'm 43 now, but I feel and look 60. Alcohol robbed me of those 17 missing future years, and most of the past 20 years is more of a blur than a memory.

"It's been six months since the last time I fell off the wagon. I'm fighting hard, but addiction fights back. I wake up dreaming that I'm drinking and I'll be drenched in sweat. When I wake up, I'm afraid I'm really drinking. I've quit so many times that I quit counting.

"Now for you younger folk, you're thinking, 'Hey, if you want to quit, just quit.' Well, I don't want to laugh at you, but hey, you ain't seen nothing yet. Just look around. It takes an army of us helping each other because this alcohol addiction thing is sneaky and mean and powerful. It's got my goat and pride many times. I'm embarrassed about it, but I've got to be honest with you.

"I've been on my new job now for three months. I'm sacking groceries, which is far from my first job in a coal mine. My uncle helped me get that job. I traded it for alcohol. Pretty stupid, huh? I'll stick with this one until I get promoted -- or if I'm sober for a year, I might begin looking for something better. That's all I got to say this time, except I do want to thank my sponsor. He's been there for me and he's pulled me back from the edge a few times in these six months. Who's next?"

Brent raised his hand. "I guess it's me. I've skipped a couple of times. Most of us have recycled through here a few times, but I've met three or four tonight whom I've never seen here before. Mostly, we're a pretty stable group. We come back for each other and ourselves because each other is about all we've got left. Most of us lost everything else we had before we hooked up here. But I've got to say, there's someone here out of place tonight. He just may be the luckiest one of us all. I want every one of you to look at who I'm pointing to." He looked Ben straight in the eye and pointed directly at him.

"Boy, did you say your name is Ben? Well, listen to our sad tales. If you've been drinking and drugging, you're one of us and you're on the same path, only you're just getting started. You're too young to drink. You can't even comprehend what it is to lose something. You've never had anything that your Pappy didn't give you, even your name and your reputation. You don't even realize that's gone, because your drug buddies still high-five you. But what about a family that matters, and friends who have stayed responsible and pursued education and careers? Do they call and invite you over or high-five you on the street? You're already losing the most important thing you'll ever have. That would be yourself and all the friends, opportunities, and accomplishments you were destined for before you took this fork in the road. You may think I'm preaching to you, but I and everyone here have a crystal ball that reads your future. We bought and paid for it, basically with our lives. It's rare as hens' teeth to see a youngster come in here, but since you're here, we're honor bound to do our dead-level best to get the message across to you that you are an addict. You're trying to deny it and fool your family as well as yourself. It won't work. Look at us. Listen to us."

"Yeah, yeahs" and "uh-huhs" were heard around the room.

"Our group is composed of blue collar people. In a town of our size, you will be shocked to see professional groups. Some are mixed; some are profession-specific. For example: doctors, attorneys, nurses, and business leaders. When addiction hooks you, it rules you no matter where you are in life. Addiction, like the fabled Smith and Wesson pistol, is the great equalizer and no less deadly.

"Judges and school counselors should send every teenager through here. We ought to have you come in here and tell us about yourself and give us all the excuses that you call reasons and rights. We would laugh you out of the room, and you're so naïve you wouldn't even understand it. I've been where you are. All of us have. I was once your age and thought I was having fun and no damage was being done to my body. After all, I could stop any time I wanted to. But a funny thing happened. I wanted to stop less and less every year. I had a good job. My boss was a good man, even like a father to me. I worked hard and made steady promotions and became the company's best foreman. I did some really good work and I won praise from my boss. He learned about my drinking and tried hard to get me to go in treatment. I thought I could handle it myself. My boss liked me and overlooked some mistakes I made, and I hid some others. His goodness enabled me to keep on drinking. Finally, I nearly cost him his company and he let me go. I betrayed the very man who loved me like the son he never had. He gave me every chance and opportunity and yet the best thing he ever did for me, and his company, was to fire me. I'll never be able to repay him for my job, or for his firing me and saving my life."

Sam thought, *This evening may well be payback enough.* His eyes moistened. He made sure not to let Ben see, but he glanced and saw that Ben's attention was intently fixed on Brent.

Brent continued, "It got worse after that. I lost my savings, my name, my car, my house, and my family. Even with those losses, I can't tell you that I won't ever have a drink again tomorrow or next week or next year. But I can tell you that I am fighting this addiction with all that I have. I learn more at every meeting. Tonight I'm accomplishing the completion of one of the twelve steps." He looked directly at Sam.

Sam surreptitiously acknowledged Brent's apology by a nod of his head. He signaled forgiveness by an inconspicuous thumbs-up. Some members were wondering why Brent was so impassioned, but they were glad.

"I feel more positive tonight about my future than at any time since the day I lost that job. A big part of that, young man, is because you are here. I look at you and realize what potential I squandered. My words tonight are coming from my heart. Seeing how young you are, I really want to reach you. As I was talking, I realized the message is for everyone who has an addiction problem, including myself. One more thing young man -- we are talking about alcohol tonight, but for many that just opens the gate to cocaine, tranquilizers, pain pills, angel dust, methamphetamines, and others. Believe me, they can bring on horrors that you can't even imagine. But under their influence and in their grip, you might yourself do these horrors. Be careful out there. The pushers are sly, crafty, and persuasive. So what do you say fellow addicts, all for one and one for all?"

Applause erupted and everyone stood and began milling around. Ben and Sam, unaccustomed to the meeting, were slower to rise.

"My name is James." An attendee spoke, approaching Ben. "It looked like Brent was taking aim at you, but don't feel singled out. He was hitting every one of us. We're just more used to it. Remember, young man, if the shoe fits, wear it. Even if it's tight and at first cramps your style, you'll get used to it if you try."

On the way home, Sam drove more slowly than usual. Brent had opened the door and this might be Sam's best chance to share those stories from Dr. Lavoy.

"Ben," Sam started, "Dr. Lavoy shared some stories with me that these guys made me remember tonight. I had decided that you were too young to hear them or believe them if you did hear them. Now I believe you need to hear them and know that these guys were being honest with us tonight. It may be strange to you, but I bet that group will go to bed happier and more content tonight, knowing that they made a strong pitch to a young man whom they might well be saving from a life of addiction."

Sam continued, "Dr. Lavoy treated a man who had a son, 22 years old, who was addicted to cocaine. The boy could not hold a job or a relationship. The son kept coming back to crash at his parents' home. He would eat, sleep, rest, and beg for money. Eventually he would be provided some cash and he would leave. His dad began cutting back on the money. The son then began stealing from his parents. When the dad mentioned things were missing and this would not be tolerated, the addicted son became indignant and argumentative, stating that it was unfair that he was being singled out as someone who might be stealing from them. The dad pointed out that he had not accused him of stealing; he was only making an observation and a statement. The dad walked into his study, hoping to disengage the conversation. The son, however, followed him into the study, demanding five hundred dollars, saying that he would get the five hundred dollars and would leave and would never bother them again. The dad refused, saying he wanted his son to stay, but he wanted the addict to leave. The son cursed him, grabbed a letter opener off the desk and lunged at him. The dad quickly took a pistol from the desk drawer and pointed it at him, and told him that he would not be intimidated by him or murdered by him for the purpose of getting drug money.

"At that point, the son leaped at the dad, plunging the letter opener into his dad's left shoulder. The dad, rather reflexively, fired the pistol straight ahead. The bullet just missed the heart, but went through the aorta leading from the heart. The son bled to death in his father's arms even before the 911 team could arrive. If you read the paper, Ben, or follow the news, then you know these things happen. Perhaps you're not so aware that it could be someone at your school. In fact, Ben, it could be you. Please don't let it be you.

"There's another case shared by Dr. Lavoy that you should know about. A twenty-year-old male addict was high on methamphetamine. One evening he lost his grip on sanity, judgment, and control. In a drug-induced psychosis, he raped his fifteen-year-old virgin sister. He never gave any indication that he remembered the incident and acted as if nothing ever happened. She, however, was severely traumatized. She discussed it with her parents, who at first refused to believe it. Finally, after believing it, they refused to let her mention it to him or to go to the police or press charges of any kind. Finally, they relented and let her go for counseling, but she was terribly troubled by the incident. She felt violated, unprotected, and that the drug-abusing brother was favored over herself, who had obeyed the rules and the laws and given the parents no trouble.

"It is imperative, Ben, that you know neither of these addicts would have believed that drugs and alcohol can and will do things to people, causing them to commit such horrible acts, no matter how strongly they feel that it could never happen to them. That was really a big part of what the AA members were trying to tell us tonight. Remember that addiction is stronger than the individual. I certainly learned some things there tonight. I hope you did."

"I did, Uncle Sam." Ben was unconvincing.

Sam had reason to continue. "I also want to point out another addiction truism. Addicts lie for many reasons, especially to get money to find and buy their fix, their drug of choice. For them, lying is nothing compared to the craving or withdrawal. Once people know you have an addiction problem, your word becomes meaningless. People also know that it is tough to live in recovery. So justifiably, it takes a long time to rebuild trust once you've given it over to addiction. You, Ben, are actually still experiencing this mistrust. I just thought you should be fully aware of this."

"I guess I should tell you," Ben began a disclosure. "You remember my friend Vaughn, who died? He told me about a time that he went ballistic on his dad because his dad refused to give him twenty dollars. He told me his dad fussed at him and told him he was a no-good druggie and didn't deserve to live, let alone have free drug money. So, Vaughn beat him up pretty bad."

Sam inquired, "What was his dad's side of the story?"

"Oh, that's a good point. I never heard his dad's side of the story."

"We tend not to question the ones we want to believe." Sam instructed, "It's a big mistake in all areas of life including the drug culture, business, politics, and religion. Always seek the full truth, Ben."

After a pause by both of them, Sam broke the silence. "Ben, you called Vaughn your friend when you told us about his death. Tonight when you mentioned him, you called him your friend. Was he really? Or for that matter, your other drug acquaintances -- were they actually friends? Weren't they more like partners in rebelliousness, a drug culture disrespectful of law, order, and decency? Weren't they partners in crime, Ben? They were not your friends, or even friends to each other. They were loyal only to their hedonistic pleasures, with no concern regarding the cost or discomfort to anyone as long as it was not them paying the price. Friends, Ben, would be there -- would be those who truly care for you and help you work recovery. Enemies work the addiction trade, and you are nothing more than their tool and pigeon."

"Gosh, Uncle Sam, I've got so much to learn."

"If you don't, Ben, it's going to be destruction and death."

"I'm glad you took me tonight, Uncle Sam."

"I'm glad we did it together, Ben."

Both were emotionally drained, yet feeling a closer bond.

The following morning as they were finishing breakfast, Ben surprised Sam with a question. "Those stories last night from Dr. Lavoy made me do some thinking. I was wondering if there is anything else that Dr. Lavoy has told you that I should know."

Surprised, but calm in his response, Sam began, "I am impressed that you want to learn. That's part of recovery. That's essential for recovery. And yes, there is one more thing that I've not discussed with you that is quite important for you and others to know. It's called co-morbidity. It really got to your father. That means more than one illness at the same time. Probably 50 percent of people with alcoholism have a co-morbid mental illness. Your father, for example, has bipolar disorder. He had some early signs of that, with some emotional instability, and he found that drinking made him forget some of the instability. However, as he continued to drink he became addicted to alcohol. That tended not to satisfy him fully, so he began using other drugs as well: marijuana, and then later, narcotics. What you need to know is that often people who have a mental illness such as bipolar disorder, depression, obsessive-compulsive disorder, or panic disorder, schizophrenia, or schizo-affective disorder will try some of these street drugs to allay some of the discomfort they have with these illnesses. While it might appear to be working initially, it is digging its hook into the individual so that the person often becomes addicted. Then they have two illnesses, or they have co-morbid illnesses.

"A particularly sad feature of this is that therapists in the medical profession tend to look at whichever one is presented. If a person comes in an acute drug or alcohol situation, the underlying illness may be overlooked. It is the same way in drug and alcohol treatment programs, even more so than in the medical field. Often a person's underlying mental illness will go five or more years before it is discovered, even after the person has entered treatment looking for help. One of the main reasons to tell you this is because bipolar is inherited and you are at a young age and may have the disorder and not yet know it. Drug and alcohol use tends to make the co-morbid illnesses worse and more difficult to treat. If someone has a family history of a mental illness, any of the ones I mentioned, the treating professional should carefully consider that history as a possible signal to an underlying illness in the individual being evaluated. For full return to a good quality of life, both illnesses must be treated. Sometimes they can be treated simultaneously; in other situations they have to be treated individually. You should read up on illnesses that run in your family. For you, you need to read up on bipolar disorder. Yes, Ben, Dr. Lavoy had told me to be sure to tell you about co-morbidity. We can discuss it further if you have any questions."

"I didn't know that." Ben seemed genuinely surprised.

"Although you've learned a lot, Ben, you still have much more to learn."

CHAPTER 29

Letter to Darla©

HELLO DARLA,

Your mother tells me that you will be graduating in May. Congratulations! It's wonderful to acquire a wealth of knowledge in just four short years of college. I'm very proud of you. Your education is a firm foundation for whatever inspired or momentous life you envision building.

Life in college gives you both good and bad knowledge, good and bad role models, and even good and bad experiences. Often the bad is cleverly portrayed and disguised as good. The young and the very old are typically the most beguiled and ensnared. The wise and mature among us are entrusted to protect both young and old. The young claim overprotection and mistrust, while the old feel betrayed by ungrateful children. How can one find the wisdom to build an adequate, desirable, useful *bridge* from youthfulness to adult maturity or from maturity to the geriatric stage? The former I must now address with you. The latter will come some other day and time.

First, timing is important. You need to be informed of the existence of a user-friendly bridge prior to embarking on your life journey.

Second, you must be reminded to seek and recognize that the bridge is an alternate, but highly beneficial course from the typical individualistic path. An entire treatise could be written on this aspect alone. Suffice it to say, this letter is meant to be timely at the present, but the nature of this letter is also to be timely when reread in a different setting or frame of mind.

Third, trust is essential. If you are to use a bridge, you need to trust the engineers and builders. Trust is gauged by long-term acquaintance, reputation, character, and credentials. The bridge builder should have a record of honesty.

Fourth, the bridge must be an acceptable path. An impossible bridge is no bridge at all.

Fifth, the bridge must have a desirable destination. A bridge to nowhere is pointless.

Sixth, there must be hope and assured assistance to those willing to cross the bridge. You should know to whom you can turn for unfailing aid.

Seventh, anything detrimental to crossing the bridge should be left behind. Previously collected harmful or dangerous baggage will prevent a successful bridging to healthy maturity.

Now, Darla, allow me to be a bridge builder. Why? During the next phase of your life, that third decade, you will make personal choices of singular importance that will be pivotal to how the remainder of your life will unfold. Consider the following anchor points. Will you live a spiritual life? Whom will you marry? Will you extend your formal education? For whom will you work? Will it be for yourself, a company or industry, or the government? Will you smoke, drink, or do recreational drugs?

Twenty-four hours after graduation, you will begin your transition from student to adult citizen, from college to independent work and life. You may choose an individual path of personal trial and error. Alternately, you could choose a solid time-tested bridge prepared and sustained by your loved ones. Please be fully cognizant that the path or bridge you choose is only the beginning of a journey that will last many years. Each decision determines your ultimate destinations. So please make sure your bridge or path is the right one for you.

What is your vision for the other end of the bridge? Do you visualize it with the foregoing anchor points in mind? I hope so. Many of your peers will be nearsighted and choose immediate gratification rather than strategically plan their journey to a more gratifying goal.

What are the treasures you will take with you, Darla? What baggage will you choose to leave behind? Hopefully, you will abandon that which would impede your satisfactory crossing into maturity, disrupt life plans, or even destroy your health.

I and others who love and care for you, most notably your parents, would give the remainder of our lives to be able to make those choices for you. We would use all of our knowledge, experience, and learned extrapolative ability that you have not had the opportunity to develop, and which therefore remains rudimentary in your current repertoire. It is of paramount importance that you use all of your effort to foresee and project with us your potential and opportunities. We want you to see the good that you may do and gain, as well as avoid the pitfalls we know you will be facing, but which for now are beyond your horizon of expectation.

Despite the foregoing, we have chosen as family, society, culture, and government to emancipate you. As a result, some of you and your friends will fare better than we have as your predecessors. Yet some of you will do worse, some much worse. We know this because of our experiences and observations during our long journeys.

Actually, with your brightness, you have observed idols with immense talent and ability who by their unwise behavior, impulsive or premeditated, have lost their positions, jobs, reputations, families, health, or even their lives. You, therefore, being observant of those obvious headline cases, should easily recognize that they are the visible tip of the iceberg. Hence, your desire to avoid these larger and more hazardous societal and ubiquitous dangers should lead you to immediately download all useful information. It certainly was not taught in formal classes, though a simple grade would have paled in comparison to the potential impact on your life. Acquiesce to your intelligence, Darla. Be vigilant in this quest before embarking on your third decade.

You will face many substantial risks throughout your future, though they are predominantly invisible at this time. From what source might you obtain unvarnished, non-judgmental, inexpensive, reliable knowledge of these certain challenges? It's your elders, Darla; those in your circle of trust. Be clear about this. NOT YOUR PEERS! They are on the same disadvantaged elevated platform as you. Most will be, deservedly so, enjoying a backward look at their marvelous accomplishments, largely ignorant of the need or availability of a bridge to a safer future. They will step off their platform onto a poorly marked path that will force them to find their own way by time-consuming and painful trial and error. It makes one wonder if somehow the *smart* part of their brain was turned off. If you have read or listened this far, you have remained smart, and I implore you to reject foolishness. I admit and declare my elderness and, mind you, I proclaim a more active role than some. I have the credentials of traversing life's course in the trenches and, consequently, likely have just enough life left at 68 years old to warn, teach, and advise you and your friends to take the bridge instead of the path.

Do you remember coming to our home when you were small? You were the cutest little girl, and so bright. You adored your Aunt Peggy. Sometimes she would babysit you at our house, and sometimes at yours. You noticed everything. Your Aunt Kitty and I considered ourselves an extra set of grandparents for you. You were very happy and vivacious, and emulated us in all that we did. You insisted on wearing Peggy's outfits and trying out your Aunt Kitty's blush and lipstick. Any time that they would prepare a meal, you would always "help" them cook. In the same way, you would follow me through the house, pretending to smoke my cigarettes. Oh dear God, Darla, it hurts so badly looking back. I thought it was cute that you wanted to be like me. Please forgive me for my youthful ignorance and any and all negative influence I had on you. I've heard that you smoke. Please stop now! I finally quit, but it was too late, as it had already set me up for lung cancer. I lost a third of my right lung, and though I'm free of it now and praying for continued health, I know I have a 60 percent chance of recurrence. And if John Wayne couldn't beat it, what chance do the rest of us have? But even that's not all. The remainder of my lungs is emphysematous. I'll eventually have to carry around an oxygen tank everywhere I go. My arteries are prematurely brittle and my risk of a stroke or heart attack is off the chart. I've got all the bad diplomas, Darla, so I'm fully credentialed to admonish you -- but I really only plead that you listen, employ wisdom, and stop smoking now. Preserve your health. Oh, I should tell you that Peggy, living with me, saw beyond the glamour. She smelled the stale ashes and saw the burns on the carpet and table, the yellow fingers and teeth, and the bad breath. She took after Kitty, thank goodness, and never smoked. For that, I'm grateful.

Smoking is definitely harmful youthful baggage. It will ruin many aspects of your life's journey. Again, drop this baggage before attempting to cross the bridge from youth to maturity.

Darla, also leave behind alcohol, definitely never taking more than a modest amount. Your Aunt Daisy's husband started out enjoying beer with friends, and then turned to excessive drinking to block the sorrow of his child's death. So he ruined his liver and, consequently, died a young man. You can't imagine how easily addiction sucks you in and hooks you before you know it. Be careful, Darla.

And pardon me for even mentioning marijuana, cocaine, Ecstasy, and all the rest. You're quite aware of their consequences for your Uncle Thomas and his family.

I won't elaborate more here, but you're intelligent and you see the big picture. It, after all, is your turn now. You call the shots. You make the decisions. We understand you are graduating to adulthood and we're not arguing the point.

Do remember the longer you're involved in something, the more difficult it is to extricate yourself, especially addiction. Another thing to know is that addiction is so insidious. It is imperceptible at first, but eventually becomes paramount: controlling and undeniable.

Also, addiction is lifelong. Abstinence does not cure. It only stops the ever-increasing and ongoing physical damage. If you're not sure whether or not you're addicted, try abstaining for a month and see if you have any discomfort or withdrawal. If so, you have a problem.

I do realize that I have used this allotment of time to address the problem of addiction. That is simply because my focus, understandable I believe, is to atone for my life of tobacco addiction. Thus, I am reaching out to you as passionately and effectively as I know how, hoping to spare you and your friends, as much as is possible, from a similar life and fate as mine.

My appeal to you, however, is beyond this message. Please don't ignore finding elders who can guide you to the bridges associated with each of the important pivotal choice categories mentioned earlier in this letter.

Thank you for your attention. It would be an honor to your intellect, character, resolve, and life if you heed this message, drop the harmful baggage, and then cross the bridge to your future.

I humbly ask that this effort be accepted as penance for any previous negative influence on you, and that any consequential positive results will be exponential because of your and your friends' future influence on generations to come.

Much love,

Uncle Sam

CHAPTER 30

Meeting the Expert
with William Jerry Howell, MD

"Lose sobriety and lose everything."

DR. HOWELL MET with Sam and Dr. Lavoy for an in-depth interview over an extended lunch. Immediately after the introduction, Sam told Dr. Howell that Dr. Lavoy had insisted that he meet with Dr. Howell before giving any lectures on addiction. "He said you're the expert and I should get pointers from you."

> **LAVOY:** That is correct. I know you personally, and your credentials are impeccable. Your reputation for being the best extends throughout Alabama as the preeminent psychiatrist addictionologist, but Jerry, you also have national recognition and acclaim. We very much appreciate your willingness to work with us as we try to map out strategies to fight the many facets of the various addictions. Sam is our convert and has become an anti-addiction warrior extraordinaire. He and I are equally as excited about this meeting.
>
> **HOWELL:** I'm glad to do it. Welcome aboard, Mr. Robbins. Anytime I can advance the effort against addiction, I do it, but

it is always nice to have help. For me, my help or assistance is gratitude and payback to those who saved me. I can't do enough, but I try.

ROBBINS: I know what you mean. I admit I'm on a crusade, but it's because I've figured out that addiction and chemical dependence are twin assassins. I was a bull's-eye for the big C. Of course, I don't intend to let it do me in, at least not until I've done my part in this war on addiction. It's unfair and unconscionable how addictions attack our youth.

HOWELL: I like your positive attitude. We need an army of soldiers in this war. We need generals and foot soldiers alike. Trying to conquer addiction is a tough battle. There are individual, cultural, and political battlegrounds. We find ourselves fighting brothers and sisters, family and friends, business conglomerates, subversive cartels, denial, personal hedonism, and the addict's own biophysiological changes that so strongly resist a return to normal. You alluded to this dependence. People know when they cut themselves that there is going to be a scar which is permanent. What individuals don't seem to realize is when the addiction hooks them, that addiction becomes as permanent as a scar.

ROBBINS: Wow!

HOWELL: Recovery is demanding and unrelenting work. You can't let up and you can't take a time-out, but it's essential if you're going to be successful. Without recovery, I have nothing.

ROBBINS: That's powerful! Is it a mantra?

HOWELL: If it's not, it should be. Sure, I'll accept that characterization. It's my mantra. Without recovery, I have nothing. If I lose sobriety, I lose everything. That's the second part of the mantra.

ROBBINS: I really like that. I'm taking notes.

HOWELL: But Sam, I never dreamed the rewards would be so great. I have a calmness that I never had even before my initial use. The peace and freedom is wonderful, but sobriety goes beyond that. I never have to lie, and I don't have to worry about where I'll get the next fix. I never have to worry about what happened the night before, and I never have to blame someone -- anyone -- for anything that goes amiss.

The two hardest things for an addict are:

To admit I'm an addict -- quit blaming people, persons, and situations, and quit rationalizing the need to abuse alcohol or drugs.

To incessantly work recovery -- realize that your brain is *broken*. What you're doing isn't working -- reach out for help from those who are succeeding at staying clean and sober.

ROBBINS: Okay, I got it: admit addiction and work recovery.

LAVOY: It's very difficult to admit being an addict. Addiction is not something we aspire to. We don't say, "By the way, I think I'll grow up to be an addict." Addiction is much more subtle. Once we try a little of this or that just for the fun of it or the thrill or the peer acceptance, addiction stalks us until it gets its hook in us. Then we deny it. We refuse to believe that we can't handle it.

ROBBINS: That's what happened to me.

HOWELL: It happened to me as well, and basically happens to every addict similarly.

ROBBINS: How can denial be so strong?

LAVOY: Think about it. Addiction is based on some form of pleasure. Often, like yours and mine, it's linked to some form of biophysiological change, programming a need to be satisfied (i.e. needing a fix). It's a part of us. It demands satisfaction in the same way hunger drives appetite. It's that strong. So we deny that satisfying our need could be a problem. We think if only we had an endless supply without legal and social complications, everything would be great.

ROBBINS: Other people complain or interfere, right?

HOWELL: Sure, blame others. Blame, blame, blame. You don't want me to have any fun. You drive me to drink or use drugs.

If it weren't for you....You want me to be perfect. You don't understand. You're meddling. It's my life, leave me alone. The laws are stupid; they need to be changed. On and on addicts travel down the road with their justifications and rationalizations. Addicts defend against recognizing their own thoughts by zeroing in on faults of others -- sometimes only perceived faults.

ROBBINS: I know I'm guilty.

LAVOY: We all are.

HOWELL: The first big hurdle to overcome is to admit that we are addicts. It doesn't matter how we got there or even why. We can blame genetics, peer pressure, and prescriptions, but we have to admit that we're addicts, and we have to DEAL WITH IT.

ROBBINS: Even though facing the fact and admitting you are an addict is difficult, recovery is even more difficult, right?

HOWELL: You are right on target. That is the reason so few individuals succeed, or they require several attempts toward their recovery.

ROBBINS: Addicts don't want to quit in the first place.

LAVOY: It's like giving up part of ourselves. It's our source of pleasure or highs. It's our coping mechanism; not necessarily a coping skill, just a mechanism.

HOWELL: That's another point, Sam. Nothing is real in the addict's world. Everything is seen through the prism of addiction – the proverbial pink cloud. When you've got your fix, you're on your pink cloud. Nothing bothers you. As far as you're concerned, you're coping with everything and everybody. There is no reality. It's as if the world stops in relation to others, and true intimacy with oneself and others is lost.

When you're down off your pink cloud, the fix is gone and you sober up. Life stares you in the face. You realize that you actually are **not** coping. You finally learn the meaning of SOBER. It's an acronym: "Son of a bitch, everything's real."

The newly detoxed addict often thinks they are recovered. At first, they won't believe how hard it's going to be, even though you tell them. The world starts up again, and guess what? The same real-life stressors will be there, just as before. It's tough, really tough, on the addict and on the family as well.

It is all-consuming for the majority of families, especially if the family itself is not addicted or in recovery. Families can't know the depth and seriousness of the problem. Addiction is like anything else; you can't feel someone else's depression, mania, or psychosis. Therefore, you're at a disadvantage to appreciate the power it has over one's entire being.

ROBBINS: I never heard it stated like that before. Very enlightening!

HOWELL: That's reality. Recovering addicts have mountains of reality to face. For example, an addict will decide, "Okay, I'm quitting. I'm going straight. I'm sober and clean." An addict immediately expects everyone to believe and trust him. He gets indignant if they don't. You will hear him say, "If you're not going to trust me, what's the point? I might as well use." An addict tries to put a guilt trip on you for treating him like the addict he has been for years, even last week. Simultaneously, he will threaten you that he will return to using if you continue to mistrust him.

LAVOY: We see that repeatedly. Addicts swear on their mother's grave. You give them an inch, or a loan, or your credit card, or your car -- but then you quickly learn that it was a mistake.

HOWELL: Of course it is. It's naïve enabling. You want to believe them. They seem so sincere, for a couple of reasons. Often, they actually believe they have put addiction behind them because they don't understand that addiction is for life. Addiction is forever. Addicts also assume borderline personality type traits. They're thinking and acting on their immediate needs without regard to potential dangers they impose upon themselves or their relatives or you. They live in and for the moment and for themselves.

ROBBINS: Is that why addicts repeat this pattern over and over?

HOWELL: It is, but the repetition usually occurs because the enablers fall for their manipulations over and over again. The addict will persuasively say, "Yes, but I didn't plan to use. I was doing great. I didn't even want the stuff. But then I was tired or sick or my wife just chewed me out." Some use the "blame-them" excuse. "And then Joe said, 'Hey buddy, you need a lift. Have one on me. I won't tell. It will make you feel better.'" After that you hear, "I don't know why, I just let it happen. Now I know better. I can't have just one. It won't happen again." But we know that it does -- over and over.

LAVOY: That's because addicts don't work recovery. It's too hard and it takes too long.

HOWELL: That's the whole point. Addicts must TOTALLY buy into recovery. Like me, many addicts say they want to recover for their family or to keep their job. My sponsor was incredulous. He told me, "You're an educated doctor and you've been through rehab and you're spitting out clichés and platitudes, but you haven't learned a darn thing. It's not about others, it never was. It's about you. Recovery is for you. You're the addict, not them. To recover doesn't mean to recover people or things you've lost. It means to recover yourself. You lost yourself, so recover yourself. Work recovery until you win recovery. Then you have yourself back. Without recovery, you have nothing. Not even yourself. Recover, and all the other things you want will be more probable." My sponsor humbled me. I knew at that moment that I was his student and he was my recovery professor.

ROBBINS: That's powerfully strong.

HOWELL: After that, I never looked back. Working recovery was my life, and continues to be my life. But most important, life was recovery. It wasn't easy, it isn't easy. I work recovery every day of my life. Recovery is what gave me my life back.

LAVOY: Is that a big hurdle for most addicts? They don't want life back. Life was so miserable for them that they have just substituted a less obvious way to escape life than, dare I say, suicide.

HOWELL: Sure. We see that more often than we like to admit. Rehab tries hard to teach and stress a concept of comfortable sobriety. If that is not attained, relapse is nearly 100 percent. The addict's DOC (drug of choice) has both an individual and a social purpose.

LAVOY: That's a good point. And the purposes are multifaceted. For example, a smoke will give the mind a stimulus and a relief from withdrawal. It can also be used as part of a peer acceptance or even as an excuse to get out of an individual or group meeting by using it as a barrier.

HOWELL: That's so true, and the same can be said for alcohol, drugs, and most addictions. Alcohol can be a social lubricant for the introvert. But just as easily it can be a social embarrassment when social controls are overly disinhibited.

ROBBINS: So, I'm hearing that if an addict doesn't buy into recovery for himself it won't work, and sobriety needs to be comfortable.

HOWELL: That's right, but comfortable does not mean easy. Everyone, including addicts, demands balance in their lives. Without balance there is chaos.

CHAPTER 31

Recovering
with William Jerry Howell, MD

SAM PUSHED FOR more information. "I apologize that we're taking so much of your time, but could we talk more about recovery?"

Being gracious, as if time mattered not at all, Dr. Howell agreed. "Of course, that's the important thing. Recovering is a permanent state and there are things that I feel are essential to maintaining recovery. I'll just run through them, if that's okay."

> **ROBBINS:** Wonderful. Any tips, suggestions, pitfalls, or tricks of the trade would be great.
>
> **HOWELL:** Never underestimate the difficulty of working recovery.
>
> **LAVOY:** Or the strength and endurance of addiction.
>
> **HOWELL:** Right. Addiction is a disease of deception. Addicts think they can handle it. You will hear them say, "I can control it. I can handle it." They think that they are *better, smarter.* They believe *just one won't hurt.*
>
> **LAVOY:** Deception is nurtured and entrenched because in the beginning and before dependence is developed, one has no particular craving or withdrawal. So at that early stage, they do handle the substance, whether they are smoking or drink-

ing, etc. They are not yet addicted and are *handling* it. Over time that illusion morphs into a delusion of denial. The deception and seduction go hand in hand until addiction eventually hooks them.

HOWELL: That's true except for the few people who get such a tremendous high from their first use, say of cocaine, that they essentially are addicted with the initial use. It is a known fact that some addicts become addicted with that first inhalation. As with most things, addicts are individual and their timeline and path to the hook of addiction may be quite different from the person before them or after them.

LAVOY: That's part of the intangibles of one's particular genetic base and their personality.

HOWELL: Nature *and* nurture.

LAVOY: So true, and also social and educational conditioning.

ROBBINS: Okay, you guys are talking science, but I'm tracking you. That makes sense. Individual differences confound the one size fits all treatment approach.

LAVOY: That's good, Sam.

HOWELL: Well, while that's true, we have to be pragmatic. There simply are not enough resources to design an individual recovery path for each of the millions of addicts. We must provide a reliable, workable approach, proven and acceptable. The most widely recognized and accepted is the twelve-step program used in many of the addiction treatment programs. One rule: 90 meetings in 90 days for starters. Meeting after meeting after meeting. Recitation after recitation.

ROBBINS: Don't some people learn quicker and need fewer meetings?

HOWELL: Some think so, but most fail. We master most things by practice and repetition. Suppose you wanted to be a master of baking cakes. You pick up a recipe and bake one. Would it be easy, like second nature, or slow and tedious with an uncertain outcome? How good or pretty would that first cake likely turn out? But if we keep using that recipe, say 90 times, we're very likely to be very good at baking that cake. Guess what? If we quit baking for a while, our skill diminishes. The more we keep doing it the same way, the more natural it becomes. Eventually it becomes ingrained as a part of us.

Remember: recovery is not about what you have learned and can quote; it is about what you apply and do.

ROBBINS: That takes a lot of time.

HOWELL: Time filled with work and patience.

ROBBINS: I'm listening and learning. It really helps to get these thoughts into words. I look forward to putting them into some type of format.

HOWELL: There's much, much more.

ROBBINS: Tell us.

HOWELL: Again, most addicts think getting detoxed equals recovery. They expect instant reward. Addicts demand trust before they earn it. Their expectations are too high. They are accustomed to the instant fix. Seven to twenty-four days after their detox, they generally will feel better. That promotes the false sense of wellness, hence they feel recovered. Then they make the mistake of channeling their effort and energy into reclaiming their lost spouse, family, job, or friend. They miss the point. Working their losses doesn't work. Recovery is working themselves. Personal recovery is the best hope of regaining their losses.

ROBBINS: Grasping that insight must be difficult for an addict. I never realized it.

HOWELL: My sponsor knew that and kept pounding it into me until he knew that I got it. I owe him my recovery and, probably, my life. Here are some bottom line closing thoughts:

Addiction resides in the person, not in the alcohol or the drug.

Recovery is about you and for you.

Addiction is being dishonest whereas recovery is being honest.

What your spouse or others do is not and never was justification to use.

Recovery is changing yourself, not others.

Get a good sponsor. Do what he/she says.

Don't blame others and don't hold resentment.

Develop an intimate, honest relationship with yourself and with others.

Daily, look into the eyes staring you back in the mirror and take this inventory:

• Have I been honest with myself in the last 24 hours?

• Have I not had a drink or abused a drug in the past 24 hours?

• Do I like the person I am becoming as the result of being honest with myself and others in the last 24 hours and working my program of recovery?

• Have I been honest with others in the last 24 hours?

• What is my role in the events of the last 24 hours?

• Foremost, you must accept daily that the most important thing about you is that you are an alcoholic, addict, or both, and you must daily work on your recovery by contacting your sponsor, and attending meetings. If you place job, family, and situations ahead of your recovery, you will surely lose your recovery and then also whatever or whoever you place ahead of your recovery.

• Actually list the important events, people, and prospects of the next 24 hours.

• Ask yourself, what are your rewards in recovery?

• Ask what is the price of failing recovery? If you use, you lose.

• These are things every addict must learn and face.

ROBBINS: That's great stuff! You're a real pro. Anything else?

HOWELL: Remember as one's addiction is developing, there is a parallel but inverse correlation with a loss of interest in family, friends, work, and usual life activities. This is actually one way to spot when someone is becoming an addict.

Recovery is a process that takes a long time to accomplish. Your family and friends will likely take a much longer time in their warming back up to you than you expect. Accept this fact and live with it. You caused it, they didn't.

The rewards of recovery can be huge, but they may be slow in coming. An addict should not expect trust, respect, or even a circle of trusted friends to embrace or surround them immediately. And also remember that recovery needs to include a balanced life. Sobriety must be reasonably comfortable.

Later Sam reflected on the meeting and observed to Dr. Lavoy, "You know, Doc, we're blessed to have Dr. Howell as an outspoken advocate for recovery. He's a doctor, and a smart man. After experiencing addiction, he not only worked his recovery, he dedicated his life's work to others' recovery, becoming an expert in the field. We are fortunate that he has tireless energy to devote to keeping others in their recovery."

Lavoy agreed. "That's so true. Now we must do our part, not just to help recovery, but to prevent beginning experimentation and use."

CHAPTER **32**

New Beginning

SATURDAY MORNINGS WERE one of Sam's favorite times. He enjoyed a slightly later, but fuller, richer breakfast. This morning, as most, Kitty prepared scrambled eggs with Sam's being the last out of the pan, cooked well, local preserves, multigrain toast, and stone-ground grits from an antique grist mill, restored to its original function by Woody Malott, still located on a mountain stream near Rayburn Gap, Georgia. This morning she surprised him by adding strips of turkey bacon.

After blessing the food and the hands that prepared it, Sam turned to Ben.

"Ben, I want you to know I was scared to death for you to come into our home. One, for fear that I (we) would not be able to help you. Two, for what disruption or havoc you might bring to us. Strangely though, providence has a way of making unlikely paths cross. Kitty and I could not be more pleased over your having been with us these few months. We have come to love you so much and you really became part of our family. We have learned from you and are gratified that you have learned from us. Things that I have learned from you will go into my talks and my book on addiction. You will get a well-deserved autographed copy."

"Thank you, Uncle Sam. I bet you weren't as scared as I was. When I realized how strict you would be, I thought it was the end of the line for me. It turned out to be the real beginning of my life. I am so grateful to you both. It makes me think about those student exchange programs. I think everyone should have to live in someone else's home for part of their growing up. It's truly an eye-opening experience."

"It's not just for growing up; it's a reminder for us adults also. Life beyond our own four walls is so different for some others that it's difficult for us to comprehend, let alone understand. The values, the desires, the abilities, the fears, and certainly the circumstances can be so different. It gives a tangible perspective to the admonition that we should walk in the shoes of others."

Ben admitted, "I would never have even considered, let alone believed, that I could see and experience life so differently and with genuine hope. In short, it's been an awesome four and a half months."

"Your rewards are coming quicker than for most, so be careful, because that makes it seem too easy. Your addiction won't ever give up. It will try to make you rationalize that it was no big deal. If you backslide, you will think that you can stop again any time you want to. You will think you can easily rebound again; it's not that easy and it gets more difficult and dangerous each time."

"I know. I won't fall back. This feels too good to lose."

"Just remember what I said. I met with a doctor. He specializes in this. I'm going to print up his notes and give you a copy. Read them carefully. They will help you stay clean."

"Sure, glad to. Also, Uncle Sam, if you ever want me to partici- pate with you in talking to young people, I'll be glad to help."

"That's great! You're on. You're my first true convert or graduate. So, you will be moving back home. And just in the nick of time, by the way, because I'm getting ready to take my bride to Freeport, Grand Bahamas."

"I'm ready to go," Kitty chimed in. "But we hate to see you go so much more than we hated to see you come, for different reasons of course. You're a fine young man and you're lucky. You have been able to come back far enough that you actually have a chance. Never forget that addiction is forever, like a noose around your neck, a devious monster that will be your sidekick for life, just waiting for some weak moment, some opening, any opportunity to once again sink its hook back into you. Any slip-up could cost you everything, even your life."

"Thank you, Aunt Kitty. I'll never go back to that way of life. That monster took over my body, mind and soul. I know my freedom is dependent on never using again."

"You're right, Ben," Sam interjected. "Never is the right word. Never again. I'll be penning my thoughts and those of Dr. Howell to paper. I want you to familiarize yourself with all of them. Those plus your own individual perspectives will make you an effective communicator. Who knows how many lives you could save by speaking to young people before they are hooked?"

"That would be great, but I've got all that you've said and done in my heart and my head. I can't thank you enough."

"No need. Just stay clean."

"Will do."

Thomas came over later that morning and picked Ben up. He could see, sense, and feel the difference in Ben. The change had been much quicker and more dramatic than his had been. He knew this was partly due to Ben's treatment being forced much younger than his. Also, it had come in a much different fashion. It was personal, individual, and 24 hours a day. Perhaps also Uncle Sam had been the right man at the right time. He choked on emotion as he attempted to express his gratitude to Sam and Kitty.

CHAPTER **33**

Vacation

SAM HAD BEEN more eager for the Bahamas vacation than Kitty, though not by much. She was eager for the excitement of a new adventure. Sam, more than anything, wanted a break from his nonstop living, breathing, working the addiction war. The day to day tug-of-war with Ben had been extremely taxing. Fortunately, he felt it had been worth it, but it was definitely time for a break.

For Sam, nothing ever charged his battery more than private time with Kitty. He had learned that Kitty was at her best, at least for him, during exciting adventures. He wanted to make sure that no one interrupted his plan to surprise her with the Bahamas vacation they had discussed. He checked with the Clees, managers of Taino Gardens Condominiums, and verified a vacancy in one of the condominiums for a ten-day vacation. On announcing this availability to Kitty, her quick enthusiastic response provided his first excitement of the vacation. Although he would not verbalize it, they understood each other, "read each other," and gained strength from each other. Their mutual admiration was more internalized than externally apparent. They stood capable and ready always to assist each other in times of need. Vacation seemed to automatically bring all this into action.

Tacitly, they knew that each other needed the time away and time together. Sam knew that some of his best thinking and planning came during vacation excursions. Kitty knew that Sam inwardly plowed deeply, introspectively, and extrapolatively with his thinking on these relaxed trips. He much preferred writing to endless sunbathing. She would eventually be called on to listen and provide immediate then later a more reasoned feedback. She willingly gave both. Often, her comments might not even relate to something she would have considered on her own. Something in the text would draw her thought process to meaningful insights, without which Sam might have left the text rougher, less fluid, and less revealing. While this axiom of their personal interaction repeatedly played out between them, the knowledge thereof would remain unconscious. Their day to day chatter and observations, while unfolding, would not seem as important as the final outcome would represent.

The first glimpse of the island was West End. Sam pointed it out to Kitty and told her that he had read that Bahamian rum runners had a thriving business operating from West End during the Prohibition era in the United States. It was only seventy-five miles to the Florida coast.

A wide, arching approach to Grand Bahama International Airport allowed a more comprehensive view. The island was impressive, being about 100 miles long. The airport itself provided an immediate island feeling. The ample runway was uncrowded. The pilot leisurely taxied to the gate area and stopped. They deplaned directly into the open air and Bahama sun. The terminal itself stood alone, unencumbered, having no adjacent commercial properties. That conveyed a powerful subliminal message to Sam that they were there to relax. *You have found your getaway destination.* Walking off the plane was tantamount to "walking away from it all." There was no jetway, but rather an immediate step off the plane into the pleasant fresh air, under a friendly sun. In unison, Sam and Kitty took a very deep breath as if nature and relaxation were settling in on them, and restoration beginning. Their transition was underway. Immediately inside, friendly immigration agents efficiently processed them and welcomed them to the Bahamas. The adjacent room was baggage collection and customs check-in. This process was equally friendly and efficient. As the carousel began bringing everyone's bags into view, Kitty was looking over the brochures at the tourism desk. Holding a "What to Do" magazine, she declared, "Look at this, Sam! There's so much to do I don't believe we've booked enough time. We'll need to stay longer."

"Or look forward to more trips," Sam cracked.

Kitty's excitement was obvious. "There's Port Lucaya with jewelry stores, linen shops, fashion boutiques, and a straw market. It has numerous restaurants, ice cream shops, coffee shops, and a casino. There's even a perfume factory where you make your own formula.

"At Port Lucaya we could visit UNEXSO and plan an excursion to Sanctuary Bay and swim with the dolphins or take a tour boat with a group to dive with the dolphins in deeper waters. It looks like there are glass-bottom boats for viewing the coral reefs and sailboats for sunset cruises. There are even charter boats for fishing trips. Across the road from the Port Lucayan Marketplace there are hotels on the beach, a spa, a wedding pavilion, swimming pools, tennis courts and several golf courses. You'll be impressed how many golf courses there are. Also on the island we could visit the Rand Nature Centre, the Garden of the Groves, or the Lucayan National Park. I'm looking forward to trying these restaurants."

"We'll get to our share," Sam obliged. He took the bags the fifteen feet to the customs agents. He answered their few questions and watched them affix their neat little Bahama label to their bags. They were encouraged to enjoy their stay in the Bahamas and shown the exit, another mere fifteen feet away. Through the door, they were now officially processed into the Bahamas, and their vacation was underway.

CHAPTER 34

Norma

THROUGH THE DOORWAY, there were friendly skycaps, taxis, warm sunshine, and a friendly-looking lady, all the more attractive because of her smile, holding a hand sign for Sam and Kitty to see, "Taino welcomes the Robbins." She had already decided that it was them and was walking toward them. Before they could speak, she said, "Hello, I'm Norma. You are the Robbins, aren't you?" They barely managed to say yes before she was into conversation with them. She was so affable that Kitty and Norma were bonded within seconds. She walked them to the KSR car rental counter, telling them all about the nice owner before they got there. She had them to follow her to Taino Gardens Condominiums, reminding them to drive on the left, as had the KSR agent and stickers inside the car.

The condominiums consisted of eight one-bedroom units and two two-bedroom units. They were shown into a single-bedroom unit, # 312. Walking through to the balcony, they found that it overlooked the pool, boat docks, the harbor and to the left, a view of the ocean just across the street. The unit was neat, clean, and finished with a personal warmness. They learned that was a Norma touch. It had a home away from home feel, rather than a set of furniture that they knew they would find replicated in the next condo. It had taken some effort and special arrangement to be the guest of the owner, since the units typically were long-term lease units. The kitchen opened to the dining area, which was contiguous with the living area, which opened to the balcony. Quite adequate, really. The other half of the condo consisted of a generous walk-in closet, ample bath and perfectly suitable bedroom. Roll-out windows were throughout, generally providing a cooling breeze without needing to turn on the air conditioner. The grounds boasted flowers from which Norma had picked some beautiful hibiscus for the unit. They found them in the bedroom, the bathroom, and on the dining room table.

Norma instructed them on the various keys and to the location of the washroom and the restaurant across the street, and the Taino beach there by the restaurant, a good place to take a nice walk on the beach. Likewise, she gave tips on where to shop, what they should expect, her phone number, and how to access long distance if necessary.

"Oh, by the way," said Norma, "you must be tired and unless you just want to go out, I've left some things in the fridge for you. There's some chicken I've cooked, a potato salad, and a fresh fruit salad. You could just warm up the chicken."

Kitty and Sam in unison, "You shouldn't have done that, Norma."

"It was nothing. I hope you enjoy it. By the way, when you are driving you will come to roundabouts. I don't think you have them in the States. You will enter on the outside. Stay on the outside to exit at the next opportunity. Stay on the inside to go round. You will get used to them quickly and you will see how much time and petrol they save. You will see that the petrol is quite a lot higher here than in the States. Adrian and I would like to have you over for dinner on Thursday or Friday evening if that would be okay. Please let us know which is more convenient. We quite enjoy getting to know people from everywhere, you know."

Sam and Kitty had been smitten by Freeport's queen of charm. Kitty commented that the encounter had been reminiscent of their stay at the nostalgic Magnolia Springs Bed and Breakfast outside Mobile, Alabama. They both noticed that this had been their first thought of home since landing at the airport. They were obviously captivated by the island and by Norma.

Kitty was eager to get to the beach. Sam was invited to join her and even if he had wanted to, he would not have been able to get away with saying no. Across the street they went, around the restaurant and out onto the beach. Something about walking on a beach blocks out worldly stresses. The soft, gentle rushes of water to the beach and back out to sea were nature's earliest melody, played endlessly for the human soul. It could never be fully disengaged and the beaches would forever be favorite destination "getaways." As they strolled at the edge of the water, they were astounded at the emerald color and the clarity (translate cleanliness) of the water. They could see the pebbles on the bottom as clearly as on the beach. Kitty was relaxed and happy. She felt that on the beach she had Sam all to herself, pulled completely away from the struggles of family problems, addictions, phones. It was bliss. She would not interrupt it by conversation, which could in no way match the beauty and serenity of this uncrowded beach.

Sam was mindful of the fresh ocean air and drew in deep breaths as if believing it had healing, restorative value. He envisioned health and vigor returning. The solitude acted as an incubator for his writing. He needed a speech that he could adapt to any audience, any city – a speech that an audience could not ignore, which would make them identify with addicts. One that would scare them to within an inch of their lives. One that would make them truly understand addiction. But also one that would give them hope and meaningful direction, coupled with conviction and determination to overcome addiction. Thinking about it was equivalent to actually organizing the aspects of the talk. The outline was forming in his head. He was ready to get back to the unit and settle into his writing. Already Sam was drifting back to his war on addiction.

"Sam, what time is it? Norma wanted us to drop in between 4:00 and 5:00 for tea. I think we should. She's really nice."

"It's 3:45. Time to dress for tea."

CHAPTER 35

Tea with the Sparrows

BEING RESIDENT MANAGERS, Norma and Adrian occupied Unit #111. Through the sliding glass doors, lush green shrubbery, beautiful hibiscus, and palm trees heightened the island mystique. The opening framed their view and path to the pool and little cabana, beyond which they could see the tops of the boats floating in the docks.

Norma's husband, Adrian, a quick-witted man, proved to be an easy introduction with a ready smile and wonderful conversational skills. He immediately put them at ease. Norma offered them tea, crackers, cheese, grapes, and nuts. Adrian offered Corona beer and had one himself. Kitty, Norma, and Sam preferred tea, notwithstanding it being late in the day.

Sam and Adrian found much in common, about which they conversed at length. They were so engaged that Sam could only catch snippets of Norma and Kitty's conversation though they were obviously energized, animated, and laughing heartily and often.

Sam surmised that a healthy dog named Bubba, who did not move from Norma's feet, undoubtedly was special among the several rescued dogs, cats, and birds whose individual stories she enjoyed telling.

At one point, the conversation came to a surprise halt as their attention turned to the open door, where a half dozen Bahamian sparrows appeared. They momentarily seemed to take notice of strangers, but then hopped right in, obviously knowing their way to where crumbs awaited their presence. Neither the birds nor Bubba took any special notice of each other, only an acknowledged eye contact. Norma definitely had stories to tell about the birds in general, and some in particular. "They go away during the hottest summer months, don't you know, but they come back for the winter. They have perfect memory for their routine and times for their daily visits. They mingled harmoniously with the doves and the blackbirds. It's funny, only the sparrows migrate. The blackbirds and the doves are fully acclimatized and indigenous here."

Sam and Kitty later marveled to each other at how everything living seemed to flourish at the Clees' --animals and plants of all types. "How is it that they are able to remain so in touch with nature, yet are enjoying the same technologies we have in the States? How are they holding on to and holding up laughter, life, and nature, while in the States we are frantically moving from one topic or chore or stress to another?" They discussed the uniqueness of this couple from Wales living in the Bahamas, quite naturally but unwittingly providing a serendipitous gift to refocus the importance of life and doing so within the first eight hours of their vacation. The joy of their visit was even more special that this couple was from halfway around the world, yet as affable and openly sharing of everything as any next door neighbor could be.

Norma wanted to know, "Mr. Robbins, I have heard that hypnosis works well in curing people from smoking and overeating. Is that true?"

"It is a very useful tool. We don't use the word 'cure,' Norma, because addiction is never cured, only controlled. Hypnosis is a way of accessing the subconscious and the emotion and, therefore, can be a powerful tool in assisting people to break their response to the addictive craving. It can actually block the craving so that the mind does not recognize the craving. Not all people are able to undergo hypnosis, but many are. A skilled hypnotist can be very effective with these people. An unskilled or untrained hypnotist might cause undue grievance by employing unsafe or dangerous techniques."

Sam and Kitty drove into Lucaya to shop and stroll through the market area. While there, they decided to dine at Zorba's Greek Cuisine. Norma's chicken would be suitable for lunch the next day. Zorba's popularity was evident with local and tourist clientele. The hostess greeted them pleasantly and quickly showed them to a table. The service was friendly and prompt. The food was excellent: fresh, tasty, plentiful, and priced fairly with an automatic fifteen percent gratuity. It was a delightful experience.

Afterward they visited the open air Count Basie Square, which was festive with live band music. People of all ages and nationalities were dancing. Onlookers standing around often shouted in their various international languages and dialects, attempting to converse with one another. Smiles and laughter evidenced shared human interest and needs. Immediately off the square, the docks allowed visitors to stroll and view the multimillion-dollar yachts.

"Who would own one of these ostentatious ego boosters?" Sam said, perhaps unconsciously neutralizing envy.

The UNEXSO office and departure site was there by the docks. Kitty wanted to make plans to return so that she could scuba dive, swim with the dolphins, and shop.

Back at the condo, it did not take long for the realization of fatigue to catch up to them.

Sleep floated through the open windows on the gentle Atlantic breeze. They had not even thought about turning on the air conditioning. The occasional hooting of a nearby owl only added to the charm of that first night as they were falling asleep.

CHAPTER **36**

Balance

LIVELY BIRDS CHIRPING merrily woke Sam and Kitty shortly after sunrise, unusually refreshed – no doubt in part from the fresh sea breeze through the night. It was understandable that they felt livelier and had a joyous feeling which seemed to harmonize with the birds. They realized what was happening. "Sam," said Kitty, "life is lively here."

"Yes, I quite agree. It's almost as if life were dormant at home. Let's go out for breakfast."

Becky's lived up to its good reputation for a good breakfast. They decided to try the Bahamian style breakfast. Kitty was the more cautious about it, especially the Bahamian fish stew. However, she was eager to try the johnnycakes.

Groceries and supplies were purchased and taken to the unit. Then they were off to Banana Bay for a stroll on the long white beach. Walking perhaps an hour, they mostly had the beach to themselves, encountering perhaps half a dozen others. They drove back to the condo where they enjoyed the meal Norma had placed in the refrigerator. Although they tried, they were unable to recall the last time they had actually had a private morning with a stroll on the beach.

Sam, however, had begun to think about his project and already was organizing thoughts in his head. Back at the condo, he retrieved his notes and pen.

"Samuel Robbins, are you going to start working?"

"No, no. This isn't work; this is fun. I'm just going to do some writing."

"You don't smoke anymore, so quit blowing smoke."

"Okay, touché, my dear. I am trying to say we all need some balance. This is purposeful work that's also a hobby, fun, and enjoyable. It just adds to the pleasure of this little paradise."

He could not let the energized, relaxed feeling slip away without taking advantage of it. He wishfully thought if he could only open a rehab unit here on the island, treatment would surely be much easier. That would be a dream came true. Later he would realize that this line of thinking simply ignored the fact of drug problems in the islands, as anywhere else.

"You're just addicted to addiction," Kitty teased.

"It's what I do now. It's my passion. When I have thoughts and ideas, I need to capture them. Otherwise, they're gone. It's not just for me. If I can do or say anything that turns one person away from a destructive addiction, my work will be validated." Sam could not have told anyone whether or not he was defending his efforts or simply philosophizing -- maybe it was both, he thought. But then what difference did it make if the effort was for a worthwhile cause?

The following morning they drove toward East End. First they stopped at the Lucayan National Park, where they visited impressive natural caves. Another attraction was Kitty's favorite: Gold Rock Beach, which is deservedly listed as one of the top ten beaches in the world. Even so, it is uncrowded. Many top world models use the location for their beach scenes. A huge rectangular rock sits permanently just offshore, reflecting an appearance like gold when the sun is at a particular angle.

After a full morning of blessed serene beach time, they drove further toward East End until they reached High Rock. Signs guided them to Bishop's Restaurant and Bar.

For lunch they chose authentic Bahamian food instead of more familiar items that were also listed on the menu. They tried the conch fritters and agreed that no one has better conch fritters than Bishop's.

Bishop was an affable native who was a delightful host and gifted conversationalist. Bishop and his restaurant would be worth a return visit.

That afternoon Sam had decided that it was time to write his basic talk. If he could get his message organized in a manner to capture and hold the attention of those in need, he was certain that he could talk their language. He would use common addictions, such as caffeine, to make everyone understand addiction and how it hooks and holds us and why it's permanent, extrapolating to the harder, meaner, and fiercer addictions such as nicotine, narcotics, and alcohol. He would hammer them with the prevalence issues. Who does not know someone desperately addicted or having lost or losing their health, fortune, family, friends, job, or maybe even their life? If we know someone, it's personal for us to help save the friend, etc. Or, he thought, someone in my audience might be like me, a convert and a zealot, wanting to do his part to save humanity from the quicksand of addiction. The more individuals fight it their way, the deeper they sink. You have to let someone pull you out and teach you how to spot the traps along every road and learn how to get safely past them.

One would be a fool to argue with the sign and take the wrong road home. Likewise, it would be foolish for anyone to argue with their doctor and not take antibiotics for pneumonia.

We must see the fallacy in personally trying the same failed efforts repeatedly only to fail more disappointingly over and over. Wisdom has to prevail. We must become knowledgeable about our dependence and our addiction. We must enlist sponsors, those winning the war themselves and sharing their knowledge and experience and proven techniques and plan. You don't need to reinvent the wheel. Walk with someone who is comfortable in his/her sobriety and genuinely cares about you and wants you to be successful.

The talk needed to be tailored to the audience. It could be general and cover the spectrum, or specific to one substance, like opioids, alcohol, tobacco, etc.

It should be geographically relevant to the audience. Use numbers that people can relate to, can understand, and easily extrapolate. For example, the Birmingham metropolitan area is roughly one million. So, that's an easy number to use. A person in the audience can extrapolate that number downward or upward with no difficulty.

Then the meaning of addiction would need to be related. The avenues of treatment, the odds of success versus failure, and the hope for success in treatment need to be underscored. They have to be motivated. They need to be first scared, then rescued, and then given a good motivational sendoff.

CHAPTER 37

Grand Bahama Addiction

KITTY CHERISHED THE privacy of the cool breeze under the cabana. She lingered longer than intended both in and out of the water. She had, however, heeded Norma's admonition to use abundant sunscreen. "I have seen too many people burn quicker and deeper down here," Norma had warned. Rationalizing that she could use the Vitamin D, Kitty soaked in as much sun as she dared.

Back inside, Kitty interrupted Sam from his intense writing. "I looked at what to do and talked with Norma about places to dine," Kitty said matter-of-factly. "We need to make reservations at some of the places. Luciano's is a really nice French Continental restaurant at Port Lucaya. I want to try their Dover sole. Norma says it's outstanding. Giovanni's is a wonderful Italian restaurant we must try. There's an English-style pub on the mall where we can have a good lunch. Norma will meet us there one day. It happens to be across the street from the Torii Gate – the entrance to the International Bazaar. It means 'a friendly welcome.' I want to see the Xanadu where Howard Hughes isolated himself from the world which he viewed through a paranoid lens. Norma says they have a scrumptious Sunday brunch that's out of this world."

Sam knew where this conversation would end. He put up no struggle. He was only glad that he had not been responsible for doing the research. Sam knew from experience that the best way to handle situations like these was to embrace them. He produced a paper and pen and invited her to sit with him to plan out their itinerary -- when and where each of these things might fit into their schedule. It obviously became a source of comfort to have everything planned, or at least all the evenings. Then there were questions of where they would shop and for whom and for what. He found himself writing out the entire week's schedule. Kitty was more of a passive adventurist. Rather than spelunking, she would prefer a glass-bottom boat cruise or swimming with the dolphins. He thought aloud accordingly. Her hints were his commands. He had learned that what he offered proactively was more meaningful to her than what she asked for. He could not remember how many years it had taken him to figure that out. But on his list of things men should know, one was that premarital counseling should be a law and that husbands-to-be should be taught such things.

The itinerary proved helpful, as they needed to veer from it only a few times. Most notably, Norma and Adrian had invited Sam and Kitty to dinner one evening, which necessitated choosing one of the restaurants to drop. The dinner with the Clees was one of the more fun evenings that they could remember from anywhere with anyone. Both of them had a knack for telling stories and they would progressively outdo each other; mostly with island stories, completely enthralling Sam and Kitty. Sam wondered aloud if he might incorporate some of their stories into his writings, with their permission, at which point he discovered, to his delight, that Adrian was also a writer and, in fact, had created a series of children's stories and was contemplating publishing them. The meal was unsurpassed anywhere else they went, Norma being a fabulous cook.

The week went by so quickly that Sam and Kitty were stunned to find it ending. They had seen the East End and the West End of the island. They had strolled three major beaches; and of course, almost daily enjoyed Taino Beach across the street.

Grand Bahama Island had been the right place for their vacation. They were relaxed and recharged. Though they were not eager to

leave the islands, their spirits had been lifted. They would be returning home more eager and energized than when they had come. They
both sensed a kindredness here on Grand Bahama not experienced
anywhere else they had traveled. Return visits were being contemplated even as they watched the island shrinking from their vision as
the plane climbed skyward.

Not long after that, Sam turned to Kitty. "Perhaps we could share
a Grand Bahama addiction?"

Kitty responded, "I just might take you up on that."

CHAPTER **38**

Collaboration

BACK HOME, SAM'S appreciation for life had never been keener. How blessed was he despite being one who had ignored common sense and repeated warnings, including annual Smoke-Out days. He had continued to pursue his addiction to cigarettes. "Smoke, smoke that cigarette," as Freddy Fender famously and humorously sang. Yet Sam was still alive and hopefully would live much longer with good treatments, doctors, prayer, and personal health responsibility from here on out. This, after all, sort of summed up his crusade. He firmly believed that if people, especially youth, fully understood the truth about various addictions and could grasp the consequences **before** they tempted fate, maybe most of them would be smart enough to stop short of starting. Most learn about other dangers, such as playing with fire or with firearms, driving too fast, playing "chicken," Russian roulette, sniffing aerosol or glue; and they avoid them.

Sam believed that our youth should see the disastrous results, whether quick and instantaneous or slowly developed over years. He thought, *We know of so many cardiac deaths from cocaine; but sometimes it is long and drawn out causing such things as chronic obstructive lung disease (COPD), emphysema, cancer, strokes, heart attacks, cirrhosis of the liver, cancer of the liver, atrophy of the brain, or infertility. We need to take the junior high school students to see people with end-stage emphysema or lung cancer or liver failure. Young students should spend several hours with these very sick people.*

Sam decided the time was right. He had collected information from various sources. He knew what he wanted to say; he knew what his message should be. He vowed to devote his current enthusiastic energy to writing his basic speech. He wanted it to be good enough to make sure that Brian would never be tempted and Ben would never look back. He wanted those who are addicted to see and understand the inherent dangers, but also the hope of treatment and working recovery. "I'm ready to write my speech," he told Kitty.

"That's great, Sam," Kitty encouraged. "Don't forget, we decided that talks from addicts would be more effective if the enabling companion also spoke. Should I start writing my speech?"

"Good point, and besides, you will need to critique my speech; and, if you'd like, I'll critique yours."

It took each of them much longer to write even the first draft than they had anticipated. Eventually they decided on a talk for each of them, but sadly admitted that no one talk could or would reach everyone. But the need was great and the cause was right. So, they and all others who care about our youth and future should give all they have to offer.

Sam informed Dr. Lavoy that he and Kitty were writing speeches. They both wanted his tutelage regarding their approach, factual accuracy, and any constructive thoughts or advice. Lavoy was happy to oblige. He advised them to prepare speeches for a large group. From that, they would be able to adapt to any size group they might address. Lavoy purposefully did not tell them of a hope he was harboring to facilitate an Addiction Awareness Day with a giant rally. He wanted to surprise them after they finished writing their speeches, and after he was sure that the event could be arranged.

In suggested revisions for their speeches, Lavoy was liberal with including professional knowledge and statistics, as Sam had actually studied very hard and earned the right to deliver such information.

Dr. Lavoy approached four local mental health companies that worked collaboratively on addiction and other mental health problems: American Behavioral (American Behavioral Benefits Managers), specializing in tailoring and managing mental health benefits and EAPs (Employee Assistance Programs) for business companies and their employees; Bradford Health Services, specializing in drug and alcohol addiction treatment programs, both in-patient and out-patient and other mental health services; EDPM (Employee Drug Program Managers), specializing in drug testing for companies and families; and The Freedom Source, a program dedicated to the eradication of drug and alcohol addiction in the central Alabama area. He thought perhaps they would like to sponsor an addiction awareness public forum. One of the local colleges might allow use of their campus or auditorium. Public service announcements and other marketing activities would entice the public as well as personnel directors, supervisors, and client companies to participate and benefit from such a program.

Organizing the event was easier than he anticipated. It would be planned to coincide with Mental Health Week or on the annual Smoke-Out Day. The program would last from 9:00 a.m. to noon, and would provide three hours of continuing education units for those in the healthcare field. Burgers, hot dogs, fries, and drinks (obviously, non-alcoholic) would be provided afterward.

Dr. Lavoy notified Sam and Kitty of the planned event. Could they meet a grand challenge such as this? It was more than they had anticipated, and perhaps they should not be the speakers. Lavoy insisted that they would be fine. Later he surreptitiously plotted a surprise ending for Sam's talk. He enlisted Kitty's help. They planned for Sam to give the first talk of the morning, and Kitty would give her follow-up speech when Sam finished.

CHAPTER **39**

Sam's Talk

"THANK YOU FOR your generous introduction.

"Please accept my sincere thanks for this remarkable attendance. Your heterogeneity embodies quite well the one million people who populate our greater metropolitan area. I will be targeting you hard in this talk and if you're listening, I'll first scare you. After that, I'll suggest you listen even more closely. Did you know that approximately one hundred thousand Americans died too young last year and every year from alcohol-related deaths? They gave up an average of 30 precious potential years of life. Consider, if the one hundred thousand per year were all in Birmingham, in ten short years everyone in the entire metropolitan area would be dead. And that's just from one addiction, alcohol. Add smoking and other drugs, and before you know it, the numbers are staggering.

"Addiction warps the way we think, but we don't even realize it. One girl, an eighteen-year-old high school dropout whom I talked with, complained that her friend accidentally took too much cocaine and died because the expletive, lazy ambulance drivers were too slow in getting her to the hospital and the doctors were too expletive stupid to save her. That's a true story from here in Birmingham.

"My five-year-old grandson, Brian, looked me in the eye plaintively and only as an uninhibited child can do, brought me face to face with the Grim Reaper. 'Grandpa,' he said, 'are you going to die?'

You see, my friends, I'm an addict and addicts die. Some sooner than others, like Kurt Cobain, John Belushi, and perhaps Marilyn Monroe. What about you, your friends, and your loved ones? Are any of you next? I came close.

"Do we need a war on addiction? Only if we don't want to die and we don't want loved ones to die.

"Before you dismiss my question, go to Webster's and to Stedman's Medical Dictionary and look up the word 'denial.' Webster's basically says 'the act of denying; to refuse to acknowledge.' Stedman's says 'an unconscious defense mechanism used to allay anxiety by denying the existence of unpleasant conflicts, troublesome impulses, events, actions, or illness.' Most addicts are in denial, not even realizing that they indeed have been hooked by the addict monster.

"In the Birmingham area, with a population of one million people, there are over nine hundred thousand addicts. You heard right. If you're not an addict, you're a misfit. Some of them will be waiting outside for you or down the street or around the corner. They will be there to rob or kill you to get their next fix, pill, or shot. It will happen daily and an uncounted number of times during this year. Or maybe they will use a child to give your child a joint or a snort as a loss leader, a marketing tool to hook your child. Our trouble is that when we are thinking of addicts, we think of those really terrible, miserable bums, the stereotypes. We don't look closely enough in the mirror or at our neighbors. Much of the public and even some professionals think of addicts as losers, not realizing that addiction crosses all strata of society and a full 40 percent are regularly employed -- and that's just the big addictions, ignoring coffee and other socially acceptable ones.

"I'm thinking that very likely 95 percent of you are thinking you're lucky to be in that small elite group of the unaddicted. But did you have coffee this morning? More than one cup? And would you be frustrated, maybe irritable and slower-starting if you didn't have your coffee? So there you are, 85 percent of us. How many of you smoke because you love the taste of tobacco or of wearing smelly clothes? Or do you enjoy sneaking outside when the boss isn't look-ing? If you don't know, try leaving it off and check it out. No. It's really that nicotine hit to your brain. It gives instant relief and stimulus. It's characteristic of addiction: the quick, conscious, pleasurable re-ward which negates the unconscious knowledge of protracted, daily, compounding, deleterious consequences such as hardened arteries, scarred and difficult to expand lungs, heart attacks, and cancer. Thirty percent of us are tobacco addicts. Yes, I said us, even though I quit in 1995. You see, once an addict always an addict.

"After being quit for a year, I dreamed that I smoked a cigarette that was a foot long. Actually, I thought it was a pretty good cigarette, but I woke up scared that I had started smoking again. That was an addiction dream. If you're addicted to anything and have tried to stop, you've probably had them; been there, done that, and understand what I'm talking about. But you didn't really understand the biophysi-ology behind it. It's important that you know these things. That is, if you want to stay quit. Recovery is not just getting clean or detoxed. Recovery is for life and it's forever. That is the hardest part for us ad-dicts to understand. We think that when we've been clean for a few months and feel better, we have kicked the addiction. We remember that in the beginning we could handle just one. We believe we can go back to socially, recreationally having just one. *Big mistake*. After we have become addicts, we no longer have the power to control how many we have. Addiction has the power over us. Take just one and you've just lost the battle with addiction. Unfortunately, many of us learn that the hard way and more than once. Addiction never goes away. **Never.** So is there some part of never that you don't understand or believe?

"Think of addiction like an allergy. You're not allergic to or ad-dicted to something you've never been exposed to. If your body recognizes something as bad for you, like penicillin, for example, or peanuts, then your body develops a defense system. It can be fierce. You can react so strongly that you die. If you're told at twenty that you're allergic to penicillin, you know at 90 that you don't take a shot of penicillin for pneumonia.

"If your body recognizes something it likes; perhaps a whole lot, like nicotine or cocaine or alcohol, your body develops an accommodation mechanism, similar to the allergy scenario, except you're ecstatically rewarded when you take that next hit. Yes, even if you wait until you're 90, your body remembers, just like with the allergy. You absolutely must grasp this concept. **It is forever.**

"But the worst part is that your intelligence works for you in allergies to help remember and warn you of the danger, but it works against you in addiction because it remembers the proximate response of pleasure and tries to maneuver you to continue the pleasure-producing behavior irrespective of the long-term dangers. Herein lies a big difference between computers and brains. Whereas logic will prevail with the computer, pleasure can and does override logic in the human brain. Your intelligence plays tricks on you. One drink, one smoke, or one whatever won't hurt. I'll be able to control it this time; no one will know; I really need a lift right now. Your subconscious is working feverishly. You need a smoke or a drink with or after meals or sex. Even your unconscious is trying to sabotage your sobriety such as forcing a dream or a symbol of what you need.

"All these methods work tirelessly and fiercely those first few days and weeks of withdrawal, only gradually losing their influence slowly over time.

"I can't say it enough; never forget the rebound punch is present forever, just like the allergy. Remember this: addiction and allergy are the only two things about us that don't atrophy with disuse or time. Years later, allow just one smoke, one hit, and the full addictive force returns with as much force as it had the last day you used. Recovery is wiped away to nothing and you start over at ground zero. That is, if you have survived backsliding.

"Take alcoholism, for example. Drinking is so socially acceptable that denial is a plausible excuse. So it's often late in the disease before one gets serious treatment. That means the addiction is firmly entrenched. Likely, the addict already has serious biophysiological changes, but they can't feel the damage to their arteries, or brain, or skin, or liver. The brain and the liver are normally very efficient organs, but the problem is that every drink chips away at the liver and at the brain. So, eventually the brain is having lapses of concentration and memory, and the liver is less and less capable of functioning. I daresay not a one of you would toss a drink onto your computer once a day, yet you seem to think nothing of soaking your brain with a known solvent. How stupid we humans are! And that liver problem? Every drink adds a scar and finally your liver looks like a ball of scar tissue. It is called cirrhosis. When you drink, blood tests show that your liver is struggling. The enzymes are up. When you stop drinking, what's left of your liver recovers over and over. So you have no clue how much scar tissue you have. It keeps recovering and keeps functioning enough to keep you alive until you are down to about twenty percent. When you've used up 80 percent of your liver you still might get by; but if you overload your liver at that point with a little more drinking, your liver can't handle it and you die unless you get a transplant. It's a rather slow, miserable death. Many recovering alcoholics are unaware of how much liver they've used up and are a few drinks away from going past the 80 percent mark. Oh, and getting a transplant isn't all that easy, so don't count on it.

"Dr. Lavoy told me of a 29-year-old girl he watched turn yellow and die over a few weeks' time. It wasn't pretty. It happened too fast and she was unable to get a transplant. She was miserable physically and mentally, and looked horrible, and knew that she had signed her own death warrant with her last binge. It was a depressing scene for her and all of them, he said. She couldn't even go home to take care of those little unfinished details that we all would like to have time to do. Twenty-nine years old. She'd had her last drink and the only move left for her would be through the morgue to the cemetery.

"Addiction is mean stuff, folks. It kills. Even if it doesn't kill you, it destroys so much of your life. Relationships are frequent casualties. Friends go away and are replaced with other addicts. Jobs are lost, families disintegrate, and fortunes are wasted.

"Don't ignore the financial burden. Consider these numbers just for drugs and alcohol alone. The annual cost in Alabama is one billion four hundred million dollars. If one thousand dollar bills were pressed together on top of each other, they would stretch from ten yards behind the football goal post to ten yards behind the goal post at the opposite end. That is 140 yards. These numbers are for the public cost, equaling over two thousand dollars per taxpayer.

"We all think, 'It won't happen to me. I'm too smart to let that happen.' That's what the 29-year-old told Dr. Lavoy. She didn't feel the hook going in deeper and deeper day by day, and neither do we. We settle for the daily relief, preventing withdrawal or the ever lesser highs or pleasures we experience, all the time ignoring the truly meaningful value of life and family and friends. Aren't we addicts pitiful?

"I know people addicted to their computers, iPods, PDAs, clothes, and certainly shoes. Now don't laugh. How many of you have more than a hundred pairs of shoes?

"I've seen people addicted to gossip. They get their highs by putting others down. There's no end to what we get addicted to -- pornography, gambling, chocolate, nose spray, cough medicine, running, racing, lying. And what about money and power? Getting it makes you feel good, right? Getting more makes you feel better. So there you go. But withdrawal occurs if you lose it. Giving up any of these, or even just a habit, will cause anxiety and discomfort, a milder and non-life threatening form of withdrawal. Yet overdoses of some of these things don't hurt in any physical, life-threatening manner, but overdoses of some of the chemicals certainly do. However, withdrawal from alcohol causes, in some people, delirium tremens that killed many people before modern methods of detox. People die from withdrawal from barbiturates, which are an ingredient in some popular pain pills and continues to be one of the medicines used by some for withdrawal treatment of alcohol. But addictions of all types can take over your life and may lead to your downfall.

"How do we become addicts? Is it something we decide? Hardly anyone would choose to be an addict. Do you know anyone who as a child raised their hand and said, 'When I grow up, I want to be an addict.' It just doesn't happen that way.

"Some of us were disgruntled, unhappy, or rebellious as teenagers; or frustrated as young adults. Typically an acquaintance, even someone we liked, perceived us as a target of opportunity. They gave us our first gateway drug: a joint, a snort, or a drink. Did it numb our pain, or ache, or stimulate our senses? It altered our mental state. It was a temporary escape. We were told it was harmless and they could get more for us. It seemed the more we used the less it worked, but the more we needed it. Hello, ADDICTION. It comes with all its financial, social, health, and legal handicaps. This, of course, is a generalization. Each addiction has its own unique nuances. At first, we denied there was a problem, but then financial and social difficulties gave us pause because we were too afraid or embarrassed to tell anyone or ask for help.

"Even then we didn't think we were addicted. After all, we didn't have to do it every day. It was just something that made us feel better. We resisted the idea of treatment. That was beneath us. It was for the real addicts; the homeless, pitiful beggar types. We had no idea how close we were.

"If we were the lucky few, our family and our friends set an intervention trap for us. They forced us to look at ourselves through their eyes. They forced us to face the future as it would be on the addiction path versus how it could be on the recovery path. If we were lucky, they twisted our arms until we agreed to enter treatment. If we were lucky, treatment began at an inpatient setting, hospital, or residential facility. If we were lucky and smart, we listened the first time through treatment and vigorously pursued follow-up once outside the facility.

"If we were luckier, our former addict buddies would respect our treatment and desire to reform and wish us well and leave us alone. Frankly, I have not met anyone so lucky. How about you? We all know how extraordinary that would be, and highly unlikely. After all, misery loves company and they want you back in the fold. You need to get smart and avoid that trap.

"Addicts don't like being told that they can't ever have just one, that they can't be just a social drinker or an occasional smoker. They point to people they know who take pain pills or benzodiazepine tranquilizers regularly without any trouble. They need to understand the difference between addiction and dependence.

"Dependence is the body's biophysiological accommodation of a substance to such a degree that without the substance, the biophysiology works in a dysfunctional, unhealthy manner, causing withdrawal symptoms.

"Addiction is the inner powerlessness to avoid using a substance or performing a behavior that is known to be deleterious or dangerous to the person whether or not there is a dependence on the substance, but the addiction appears to be worse when coupled with dependence.

"We know, for example, that alcohol, benzodiazepines, and opiates, including cocaine, cause dependence and addiction. Sex, gambling, and computers can be highly addictive, but there's no physiological withdrawal, though psychologically one may be very unhappy and anxious in the absence of their addictive behavior.

"It remains confusing to some people, even some doctors and counselors, as to the difference between dependence and addiction. I had a friend who had an absolutely horrible back pathology documented with x-rays and MRIs. Her pain was excruciating and not relieved by over the counter pain medicines, yet by taking four tablets per day of Darvocet N 100, a combination of Tylenol with a mild synthetic narcotic, along with an antidepressant, she was able to get enough relief to tolerate the pain. Her husband told her she was addicted, yet she never escalated the amount nor went to other doctors for additional prescriptions. Her husband told her that the devil had power over her and she would go to hell if she did not quit. He was a deacon in their church and enlisted the help of the minister to drive out the demon. She stopped the pills, but after a couple of months, she could not tolerate it any longer and resumed her medication. Everyone thought it was wonderful and miraculous that she had gotten so much better. That is, until her husband found her pills and confronted her. His preaching of hellfire and damnation returned. She then took the ultimate pain reliever -- taking a bullet to the head by her own hand. The irony, of course, was that the poor woman was not an addict. She was dependent, much as a diabetic might be dependent on their insulin. Today there might have been other non-narcotic treatments that could have given her relief such as electrical stimulators, etc.

"The blur between addiction and dependence, and appropriate treatment versus drug-seeking addicts is a significant problem for pain patients and doctors. Pain patients should utilize pain clinics as much as possible to minimize these obstacles.

"If anything you've heard in this talk makes you have doubts about yourself or a loved one, read the book *Addiction: Yours, Mine, and Ours,* and perhaps the AA Bluebook. Don't ignore **addiction** or **dependence**. They are **twin assassins**. And they both are treatable. You can recover and there are ways to stay recovered. Relapse is always lurking inside, waiting for a weak moment to tempt you with the very best reasons and logic that your subconscious can muster. Don't give in.

"One subtle, murderous technique used by dependence is through tolerance. The more we use, the more our body tolerates. For example, with both alcohol and opiates the body progressively tolerates more and consequently requires more to obtain the desired effect. Since both are sedatives, they slow the body functions, specifically breathing and heart rate. Eventually the required dose can be essentially the fatal dose. Often those who are dependent as well as those who are addicts will be unaware just how closely they are flirting with death. Without giving it a second thought they might take something extra, a tranquilizer or sleeping pill. Many have done just that and drifted off never to realize that they have assassinated themselves. Addiction and dependence are twin assassins.

"Although one treatment does not necessarily fit all, we generally accept the twelve-step program to be the gold standard. It is particularly useful in alcohol and opiate addiction. It can be adapted and useful in practically every addiction. I highly recommend it.

"The single biggest mistake we make regarding treatment is thinking we can do it by ourselves without help. Who can do what they don't know how to do? Go to meetings. As they say, 90 meetings in 90 days to start. Listen and learn. Share and learn even more from those who have been there before you and, importantly, who have overcome that.

"Get a sponsor. Be thankful for your sponsor and utilize their knowledge and experience. Be grateful for their dedication. When you are ready, return the favor and become a sponsor.

"Walk the steps – each and every one.

"Don't get cocky. Don't lower your guard. Stay vigilant about recovery.

"Remember recovery is never completed. Sadly, most addicts are not smart enough or committed enough to prevent a few relapses. Some die needlessly because of that.

"My friend, Dr. Jerry Howell, a psychiatrist and addictionologist, is quoted prominently in the book *Addiction: Yours, Mine, and Ours*. He is knowledgeable and experienced. He has discussed his recovery on national television. He believes and lives the motto, 'Recovery is everything. Lose recovery and lose everything.' Addiction is all-encompassing and for some it's even life itself.

"Remember you are not stronger than addiction. Don't arm-wrestle addiction – it will win. Tell addiction that you realize that you have 'had your limit.' You will never indulge in it again. You will henceforth everyday of your life work recovery. Mean it, live it.

"Thank you for coming and for your kind attention. We have time for a few questions.

"Yes, the question is what about Chantix for smoking. It appears to work great for a number of people. You should be aware that for others it takes away most pleasure and for depressed people, therefore, it could exacerbate depression to the point of suicide. So, be careful if you venture into using Chantix."

Sam called on another audience member with a raised hand. "What about Suboxone for opiates?"

"Suboxone is different from Methadone and it is my understanding that it is working better than Methadone (dolophine) for a significant number of people. It can be prescribed by certified practitioners for dependence whereas Methadone must generally be obtained through Methadone clinics."

Someone else asked, "You mentioned early on the violence associated with addiction. Can you elaborate on that?"

"Yes, addiction in its various forms is responsible for an extreme amount of violence. Generally, it's the addict killing or robbing in an attempt to get money for more of the addictive substance. Sometimes these addicts are kids killing or robbing their parents or relatives. Occasionally, even parents will, in self-defense, kill their own children who are attacking them for drug-related needs. It causes countless automobile accidents and associated deaths and carnage. It causes meditated and unmeditated, impulsive violence.

"A good estimate of alcohol-related deaths in the United States is one hundred thousand per year. If you go online to www.heloguemd.com and click links, then select Addiction, you will find useful information about resources.

"There are a couple of other treatment options we need to mention. One is Campral. A drawback is the need to take pills three times daily. It effectively blocks the receptors that allow one to feel good from alcohol. So the incentive is taken away. Also there is a disincentive to use because one will become just as drunk, clumsy, and stupid. IF, and that is a big if, one takes the med it is a good deterrent. Another treatment is Vivitrol, a once a month injection that not only prevents the pleasure of drinking, but also helps to reduce the cravings. If you like this concept, discuss it with your doctor."

"Why aren't we making more headway on the deterrent to drugs?"

"Drug trafficking is lucrative and related to supply and demand.

As we discussed, pushers find devious ways to get hooks into new recruits. They constantly need new blood. They use cruel and clever tactics. They work in hidden areas. We don't have enough resources or a big enough army to track down all the pushers and kingpins or to put them away for life when they're convicted.

"So the answer is for people like you and me to extract the hooks from our lives, work recovery, and teach abstinence to the youth. They should fear addiction like poison. We must make them see the danger and the power that it has and will exercise over them. We must keep the youth from starting. When we teach our children convincingly enough to prevent them from trying addictive substances, we could essentially eradicate destructive addiction in three generations. We must all take responsibility. Concerned people like you and me are the only army that will win this war. Thank you for listening, and have a good life."

CHAPTER 40

Enabler No More

SAM CONTINUED, "NOW please welcome my former enabler, my wife. She says I've only told you half the story."

"Thank you, Sam. I volunteered for this not because I like public speaking. In fact, it's difficult for me. But this crusade, or war on addiction, is important to Sam; to our grandson, Brian; to all our family and friends; to every one of you, and each and every citizen. Did I leave anyone out? I didn't mean to. But please do relax. I'm not the talker Sam is. I'll be brief, though I do have a message.

"If you really want to know what's hard, I'll tell you, but I'll bet any addict out there already knows. It's quitting, when you've got a good enabler, especially one that may also be naïve.

"I personally didn't have a clue until I went to a few Al-Anon meetings. When Sam suggested I go to counseling or at least Al-Anon meetings, my response was, 'Why should I go?'" Heads were nodding throughout the audience and ripples of laughter created a small pause.

"And then I added, 'After all, it's your problem.'" Further laughter.

"Was I ever the fool! I made it so easy for Sam. I purchased his cigarettes by the carton during *my* shopping at the grocery store. I always kept a pack hidden just in case he ran out. I started one day after Sam had gotten up in the night and driven to 7-Eleven for a pack of cigarettes. I even swapped it out from time to time so that he wouldn't get a stale pack.

"Whatever made Sam happy, that was my job. If he mentioned quitting, I voiced agreement and happiness, but Sam knew I would have that emergency pack waiting to rescue him. When anyone mentioned Sam's smoking, I would downplay it. 'It hasn't seemed to bother Sam,' I would say. 'I've gotten used to it, so I hardly notice.' Was I also in a little denial? I was what's called a full-fledged enabler. I never complained. In fact, sometimes if he seemed moody or irritable, I would suggest he go for a smoke.

"Enablers are not all alike. Some, in fact, do complain and argue routinely, at which the addict can self-righteously complain, 'You're the reason I drink; you drove me to drink.' Other enablers will be mad at the addict, so they will deliberately do things to irritate him. And naturally, he has to then find a tranquilizer -- be it liquid, smoke, powder, whatever. If someone in your family is an addict, don't put off another day going to find out how your actions, or inactions, are a big part of the reason -- or at least an enabling factor -- in their behavior.

"For help, go to Al-Anon (http://www.al-anon.alateen.org/) or Narc-Anon (http://www.na.org/). The National Institute on Drug abuse (http://www.nida.nih.gov/) and the National Institute on Alcohol Abuse and Alcoholism (http://www.niaaa.nih.gov/) also provide valuable knowledge and resources.

"We make excuses in our enabler role. Have you heard anything like this before?

"I love her.

"I don't want to hurt him.

"What would I do if he left?

"What would his leaving do to the children?

"He drinks too much, I know, but he's a good provider.

"The kids love him.

"What would people think if I left him?

"He needs me.

"He loves me.

"And for sure, there are hundreds more *good reasons* that we enable.

"But once in a while we will find a less altruistic reason to enable.

There's always one I like to point out. Hopefully it's not your enabler, but you might hear them confiding to a friend or their psychiatrist, 'He makes my life miserable. I figure, what the heck, the more I can get him to drink, the sooner he croaks.'" That evoked some laughter, but rather telling, a few groans also.

"So you see, enabling is a complex behavior, but a truly integral part to the addictive process. The main point of my being here is to reinforce the need for addicts to figure out who their enablers are and make sure they are fully incorporated into the recovery plan. If they're not, they're likely to conspire with the monster within you to trick you into losing recovery and losing everything. After all, if you get irritable, they know what will soothe you and calm you down, right?

"Well, now it's up to you. You need to upload everything you've heard from us, click on 'run,' and never look back. Did you ever notice addicts wearing butterfly pins? Addiction has a butterfly effect. It flaps its wings in Africa and causes a storm in America. One addict has enormous far-reaching destructive potential.

"Admit that you have a problem, detox, sober up, begin recovery, and then live. In that order.

"Detox thoroughly.

"Sober up. It's more than detox.

"Work recovery. It's much more than being sober.

"Live a comfortable sobriety.

"Make sure your new friends are monster-killers.

"When you're strong, be someone else's monster-killer.

"Never again be an enabler.

"Good luck, God bless you -- and think twice about the manner of help you give to an addict."

CHAPTER 41

Monster Awards

AFTER HER SPEECH, Kitty did not return to her seat as Sam had expected. Instead, she motioned for an unexpected guest to come say a few words. She introduced Ben, their nephew. Kitty told the audience, "This is Sam's and my nephew, Ben. We had the pleasure of him living with us a few months last spring. He asked to join us on stage. It is my pleasure to introduce him."

"My name is Ben Robbins and I'm an addict, the hard-core type: you know, alcohol, opiates, and benzos. I was a dead man until I learned to live while staying with Aunt Kitty and Uncle Sam. Dead in my soul, my life, my family. You know what I mean. My body kept on going and going, but only to find more booze and dope. Everyday I was closer to the cemetery or prison, but didn't realize it. Aunt Kitty and Uncle Sam intervened at the request of my parents and against my wishes. They refused to let me fall into that grave. After they sobered me up and cleaned me out, they showed me my potential in recovery. They also showed me the danger ahead on my addiction path. They showed me how to believe in myself and work recovery. I owe my life to them.

"I'm here to tell anyone who will listen, if you have never used then don't start. If you have, stop now. Get all the help you need and work recovery every day. Don't let your friends use. It's like letting a stupid or ignorant kid play with a loaded gun.

"One of my drug friends, a lawyer's son, died last month of an accidental overdose. He thought he was getting high. He didn't realize he was killing himself.

"Another friend, a doctor's son, is strung out on drugs and is in detox. Another friend, a minister's son, just recently finished a rehab course at Bradford and he is currently clean. Like me, he faces a life of working recovery to stay clean.

"Thank you for letting me give you this warning, but especially let me publicly thank Aunt Kitty and Uncle Sam."

Kitty asked Ben to stay there and motioned for Sam to come back to the podium. She and Dr. Lavoy had planned this little surprise. Dr. Lavoy came forward and elaborated on how impressed he was with the work Sam and Kitty were beginning and how much he was enjoying working with them. They had come up with an idea of addiction monsters, so he had commissioned an artist to design these hook monsters. Holding one up, he said, "The monster's left hand is replaced with a hook poised ever to strike you unless you somehow disable it. When you detox and enter recovery, you are refusing to be bothered by the hook. And so, you remove the monster's hat and place it where it conveniently covers, hides, and disables the hook.

"Sam, the hat on monster number one has the name Smoky written on it. You are hereby awarded the number one, Smoky hook monster. And by virtue of your long abstinence, you are given permission to remove the hat and disable your monster."

Sam, more emotional than he wanted to be, was tearing up, betraying his manhood. Nevertheless, he showed the audience he was definitely covering the hook.

Dr. Lavoy handed Sam another monster, advising him that he should present this one to Ben as he was now several months into recovery. And it should be noted by all that the name on his hat was Poly, signifying poly-substance abuse.

Sam happily obliged and made the presentation. He proclaimed that Ben's entering the recovery process had been his proudest moment since beginning the addiction eradication crusade.

Ben was shocked. "I can't believe this. Thank you. This monster will stare me in the face every day the rest of my life. I will keep him disabled."

"Ben," said Sam, "I say that anyone with a hook monster can't hide the hook until they are clean for 90 days. If we slip, the hat goes back on the head, unleashing the hook until we have again been clean for at least 90 days."

Suddenly, Brian came running onto the stage, surprising everyone. His voice carried out over the PA system. "Grandpa, I want a monster. I'm clean. I'm never going to smoke."

Sam visibly radiated pride and surprise. This is exactly how it needs to be. If we can teach this generation, they will teach the next and the next. "Brian," said Sam, "we'll get you a monster. We'll name it *Free* because you are unspoiled by any addiction. As long as you are addiction free, your monster will have no hook. May your monster never develop a hook."

Addiction Statistics

Addiction	Prevalence	Cost to Economy	Annual Number of Deaths
Tobacco	70.9 million	$130 billion	440,000
Alcohol	14 million	$185 billion	85,000
Prescription Drug Abuse	6.9 million	$181 billion	20,000
Illicit Drug Use	20.4 million	$215 billion	20,000
Cocaine	3.6 million	$36 billion	5619
Opiates	2.4 million	$20 billion	5315
Heroin	213,000	$17 billion	1893
Sex	21 million	N/A	N/A
Gambling	3 million	$40 billion	N/A

National Institute on Drug Abuse - www.drugabuse.gov

Centers for Disease Control WONDER Mortality Database – www.cdc.gov

Addiction is...

1. for everyone. No one is naturally immune.
2. a permanent condition.
3. resilient and will instantly bounce back with full force.
4. a mighty adversary of recovery.
5. found everywhere.
6. found in almost everything, from shoes to heroin.
7. tenacious; determined to keep you.
8. knowledgeable of every trick to fight recovery.
9. clever in using your subconscious and your unconscious against you.
10. going to cost you everything you have.
11. going to alienate your family and your friends.
12. going to kill friends and possibly you.
13. your unlucky fate.

Recovery is...

1. possible.
2. difficult for most addicts.
3. minute to minute, day to day, month to month, year to year. In fact, lifelong.
4. everything. "Lose recovery, lose everything."
5. an opportunity for you.
6. hope you can believe in.
7. a solid answer for the fully committed.
8. best with professional guidance.
9. safer with an experienced, dedicated, caring buddy or sponsor.
10. living clean and better.
11. a respected accomplishment.
12. yours to earn and maintain.
13. your lucky answer.

Internet Resources

H.E. Logue, M.D. – www.heloguemd.com (for quick links)

Al-Anon – www.Alanon.org

Alcoholics Anonymous – http://www.aa.org

American Academy of Addiction Psychiatry – www.aaap.org

Bradford Health Services – www.bradfordhealth.com

Cocaine Anonymous – www.ca.org

Gamblers Anonymous – www.gamblersanonymous.org

Narcotics Anonymous – www.na.org

National Center on Addiction and Substance Abuse at Columbia University (CASA) - www.casacolumbia.org

National Council on Alcoholism and Drug Dependence, Inc. (NCADD) – www.ncadd.org

National Council on Sexual Addiction and Compulsivity – www.ncsac.org

National Institute on Alcohol Abuse and Alcoholism (NIAAA) – www.niaaa.nih.gov

National Institute on Drug Abuse (NIDA) – www.drugabuse.gov

The Chris Sidle Foundation – www.thechrissidlefoundation.org

The Freedom Source – www.thefreedomsource.com

Recommended Reading

Alcoholics Anonymous. (2001). *Alcoholics anonymous: Big book 4th edition*. New York: Alcoholics Anonymous World Services, Inc.

Alcoholics Anonymous. (2001). *Twelve steps and twelve traditions*. New York: Alcoholics Anonymous World Services, Inc.

Beattie, M. (1992). *Codependent no more: How to stop controlling others and start caring for yourself*. Center City, MN: Hazelden Foundation.

Califano, J. A. (2007). *High Society: How substance abuse ravages America and what to do about it*. New York: PublicAffairs.

Carnes, P. (2001). *Out of the shadows: Understanding sexual addiction*. Center City, MN: Hazelden Foundation.

Cole, B. S. (2000). *Gifts of sobriety*. Center City, MN: Hazelden Foundation.

Conyers, B. (2003). *Addict in the family*. Center City, MN: Hazelden Foundation.

Drews, T. R. (1998). *Getting them sober: You can help!* Baltimore: Recovery Communications.

Doidge, N. (2007). *The brain that changes itself: Stories of personal triumph from the frontiers of brain science.* New York: Viking Press.

Dupont, R. L. (2000). *The selfish brain: Learning addiction.* Center City, MN: Hazelden Foundation.

Fletcher, M. (2002). *Sober for good: New solutions for drinking problems – advice from those who have succeeded.* New York: Houghton Mifflin Harcourt.

Hoffman, J., & Froemke, S. (Eds.). (2007). *Addiction: Why can't they just stop?* New York: Rodale Books.

Jampolsky, L. (1991). *Healing the addictive mind.* Berkeley, CA: Celestial Arts.

Johnson, V. E. (1990). *I'll quit tomorrow: A practical guide to alcoholism treatment.* New York: HarperOne.

Milam, J., & Ketcham, K. (1984). *Under the influence: A guide to the myths and realities of alcoholism.* New York: Bantam Books.

Nakken, C. (1996). *The addictive personality.* Center City, MN: Hazelden Foundation.

Narcotics Anonymous. (1991). *Narcotics anonymous.* Center City, MN: Hazelden Publishing and Eductational Services.

Reid, R. G. (2007). *Recover all.* Eugene, OR: Wipf & Stock Publishers.

Stromberg, G., & Merrill, J. (2005). *The harder they fall: Celebrities tell their real-life stories of addiction and recovery.* Center City, MN: Hazelden Foundation.

Twerski, A. J. (1997). *Addictive thinking: Understanding self-deception.* Center City, MN: Hazelden Foundation.

West, J. (1997). *The Betty Ford Center book of answers: Hope and help for those struggling with substance abuse and for those who love them.* New York: Pocket Books.

About the Author and His Books

FLY ME TO the Moon: Bipolar Journey through Mania and Depression won an EVVY Merit Award from the Colorado Independent Publisher's Association in 2007. This was Dr. Logue's first novel to begin a series to demystify mental illnesses for the public. The book has received wide acclaim and has set the stage for the following books. This second book is *ADDICTION: Yours, Mine, and Ours*. You will finally understand addiction and its treatment.

Dr. Logue graduated from the Medical College of Georgia in 1963. Following an internship at the University Hospital in Augusta, Georgia, he practiced general and family medicine for five years. Dr. Logue returned to the Medical College of Georgia for a three-year accredited psychiatric program and after completion he moved to Birmingham, Alabama where he has enjoyed a satisfying career.

In 1974, Dr. Logue organized and opened a psychiatric unit at a major Birmingham hospital. He chaired that department for twelve years and grew it to a 96-bed psychiatric department. He currently is the director of the geriatric behavioral health unit at Baptist Medical Center Princeton in Birmingham, Alabama. His office practice is at Affiliated Mental Health Services in the Birmingham area. He co-founded American Behavioral Benefits Managers, Inc., a noted mental health benefits company serving patients in all 50 states and Canada.

His first novel remains the only novel to be approved for continuing medical education credits for the medical community. He received the Exemplary Psychiatrist Award from the National Alliance on Mental Illness (NAMI).

At his web site, www.heloguemd.com, you can view his brief or extended bio as well as find links to informative sites on the mental illnesses. To schedule speaking engagements by Dr. Logue, contact Peggy at (205) 978-7830.

LaVergne, TN USA
05 January 2011
211088LV00004B/54/P